CRACKPOT

Books by Ron Goulart

Science Fiction/

THE SWORD SWALLOWER
THE FIRE EATER
GADGET MAN
AFTER THINGS FELL APART
DEATH CELL
PLUNDER
CLOCKWORK'S PIRATES
HAWKSHAW
WILDSMITH
SHAGGY PLANET
A TALENT FOR THE INVISIBLE
THE TIN ANGEL
FLUX
SPACEHAWK, INC.
WHEN THE WAKER SLEEPS
THE ENORMOUS HOURGLASS
THE HELLHOUND PROJECT
A WHIFF OF MADNESS
QUEST OF THE GYPSY
THE EMPEROR OF THE LAST DAYS
THE PANCHRONICON PLOT

CRACKPOT

RON GOULART

DOUBLEDAY & COMPANY, INC.
GARDEN CITY, NEW YORK 1977

HOUSTON PUBLIC LIBRARY

All of the characters in the book
are fictitious, and any resemblance
to actual persons, living or dead,
is purely coincidental.

Library of Congress Cataloging in Publication Data

Goulart, Ron, 1933–
Crackpot.

I. Title.
PZ4.G692Cr   [PS3557.085]   813'.5'4
ISBN: 0-385-11640-3
Library of Congress Catalog Card Number 76–23764

CRACKPOT

CHAPTER ONE

These things all happened at approximately the same time on June 13, 2015.

In the Connecticut Colony it was a few minutes after 11 A.M. when the lanky bald-headed young man in the threadbare World War III uniform came shuffling up to the gates of the Fairfield County Executives Country Club Hospital. He had several cuts and gashes on his gaunt sooty face; some healed, some that-morning fresh. His synthskin boots were of different sizes and both meant for the left foot. Apparently his most recent tussle had left him slightly giddy. He shuffled along the plyolawn path in wide tottering arcs, bumping against a decorative pine at the right of the road, then stumbling into a mechanical watchdog on the left-hand side.

None of the dozen fierce-faced robot dogs barked, or even bristled.

The battered young man tottered on. In his grimy right fist, which his shredded trouser pocket only partially concealed, he held an object about the size of a pool ball. It was white and had ten white protruding knobs. As he shambled closer to the gates the bedraggled young man depressed another of the knobs.

A glistening white-enameled android came striding out of the gatehouse. "Yes, sir?" he smiled, opening the pseudoiron gates wide.

"I feel hacky," complained the young man. "I got snarfed down in the Westport Shanty Town . . . bastards tried to moog my Gadget but I held on . . . want to get patched up now."

"Most certainly, sir," said the android sympathetically. "The Fairfield County Executives Country Club Hospital was built expressly for important people such as yourself."

"I got to take a weep pretty bad, too," said the scruffy young man. "Is it okay if I rack off on your decorative lawn here?"

"Certainly, sir. Help yourself." The android gestured invitingly at the five acres of synthetic vinyl grass which stretched from the hospital's real stone wall to its cluster of buildings. "While you're relieving yourself, I'll fill out an entry report."

"Sure thing." The young man's trousers were sufficiently tattered so that he didn't have to unseam them.

There was an impressive view of the surrounding area from the lawn. You could see a vast spread of estates and villas and then, some three miles off, the woodland-integrated National Robot & Android facility.

"Name, sir?"

"Huh?"

"Your name is . . . ?"

"They call me Turkey."

"That's fine. Name: Turkey. And which of Connecticut Colony's thriving firms are you affiliated with, sir?"

"Does that mean what I do for a living?"

"Exactly, sir."

"I moog voxgram transmitters. Sell 'em to a fence in Jersey Colony."

"Very good. Occupation: thief." The android nodded his white-painted head. "Now I'll summon a servochair to wheel you to your treatment suite, sir."

"Swell." Turkey pushed another button on the white sphere.

The fat girl headed for the Omaha Freemat at about 10 A.M. Heartland Empire Time. She was twenty-two years old and enormous, there was at least three hundred pounds of her.

Two yeomen floating by on a hayrover watched her go swaying up the ramp of the silo-shaped Freemat.

"The andies'll toss her out on her bummy, Yeoman Kolb."

"She'll bounce something terrific, Yeoman Lumbard."

The fat girl had one plump hand hidden away in the folds of her fruit-pattern lycra shift. In that hand was clutched a round white object with ten projecting knobs. "I'm starving," she told the red-white-and-blue robot stationed at the edge of the forcescreen hatchway.

"Poor child," clucked the robot, who had no head and four arms. "Go right on in before you collapse."

The forcescreen blinked off, and the fat girl charged across the threshold and into the Freemat.

"Please have your Heartland Empire Welfare Tattoo number ready to show," instructed the handsome flesh-tone android seated on a floating stool near the right-hand food wall.

The fat girl pressed a button on the white ball. "My number faded off, but that's okey dokey, isn't it?" she asked the handsome andy.

"Why of course, of course. You can go over to the walls and order whatever your little heart desires."

"Much obliged." She went hurtling to the dessert wall and commenced pointing at the see-through slots. "One of those . . . two of those . . . one of those . . . a half doz of these . . ."

The black man put the wine pouch to his cracked lips. "Um yum . . . mighty good. You bet." He staggered out of the #16 passenger kiosk at the Frisco Enclave Municipal Airport and made his way to a forcefence cruiser pad. It was a few minutes beyond 8 A.M. Liberal Pacific Time. There were seven cruisers parked on the pad. Weaving, the black man tilted the pouch to his mouth once again. "Yum um. That's surely mighty good. Pineapple and tropical fruit make the best doggone wine. You bet." In his left hand, which was stuffed in the coat pocket of his homemade sacking suit, he held a white ball about the size of a billiard ball. The sphere had ten protruding knobs on its surface.

Two blue-steel guard robots were stationed immediately in front of the cruiser pad. "Halt!" they simultaneously ordered the staggering black man.

"Just let me get my mojo working . . ." He pushed down two of the knobs. "Now then, my good man . . . my good men . . . I wish my special air cruiser readied."

"Yes, of course, sir." Both of the seven-foot-tall robots bowed. "Which air cruiser is yours, sir, if you please?"

The Negro blinked, took another sip of his fruit wine. "I see you do not recognize me . . . I happens to be the Finance Minister of the Republic of Southern California."

"Forgive us, sir. We were led to believe you wouldn't arrive until nine."

"Yeah, that's what it say on the news . . . but I decided

to sneak away a little bit early. That's my cruiser there, ain't it? The big crimson mother."

"Yes, that's the one the enclave government has provided for you," replied both the big robots. They pointed at the forcefence and an opening appeared. "Allow us to escort you to the craft."

"Much obliged."

"And where would you like the vehicle to take you, sir?"

"Oh, just circle round for a while . . . then maybe later we can take us a little jaunt up to the wine country."

The simulated grandfather clock in the Fun House parlor was chiming 8:15 A.M. Conservative Pacific Time when the small long-bearded old man made his way, slowly and carefully, into the oval room. He wasn't an inch taller than five feet and was nearly ninety. His wardrobe consisted of a pair of GI polyester sleep pantaloons and a poncho cut from a Veterans' Enclave Hospital blanket.

"Yeah?" A tabletop reception box turned its scanning light on him.

Under the tacky blanket the old man clutched a white knobby ball in his scrawny hands. He shoved in a button. "I'm here to kick up my heels! Sew a few wild oats! Reap the wild wind!"

"Sure thing," said the reception box cordially. "What's your pleasure, sir?"

"I'm seeking a little nookie! I want to get my ashes . . ." The old man suddenly dropped down onto one of the room's plastic nineteenth-century-style sofas. "All this excitement is taking its toll."

"We got lovely nubile female androids representing all the races and creeds in what's left of the world," explained the reception box from its claw-footed table. "We also got intellectual type female androids built like militant Frisco Enclave dames. We got cornfed bumptious beauties who you'd swear were fresh off Heartland Empire food farms. We got—"

"Haven't been off the grounds since back in '99." The old man was slumping farther down into the sofa. "Been thinking about women all that time, but they never let me near one . . . been thinking about quiff since 1999, and then I finally persuaded my ungrateful great-grandnephew to get me a Gadget and smuggle it in . . . well, sir, I made up my mind I was going to really . . ."

He fell forward onto the synthetic persian rug, coughed once and expired. His right hand had emerged from under the poncho. The gnarled fingers relaxed in death and the white knobby ball went rolling from his grasp.

It rolled all the way across the reception parlor and out into the corridor.

That was where Rafe Santana saw a Gadget for the first time.

CHAPTER TWO

From the Fun House corridor Rafe Santana watched as a panel in the parlor wall slid open. Two medirobots wheeled out to grab up the collapsed old man.

Rafe knelt to reach for the Gadget.

As his fingertips touched it a voice from down the corridor suggested, "Leave it be, greaser."

Rafe was a long lean young man of twenty-nine. He picked up the white ball, straightened to his full height. "Beg pardon? I thought I heard you make a reference to—"

"Give that here, spic!" The android was big and wide. He came swaying down the soft-lit corridor.

"I've never dismantled an android before, but if—"

"Easy, Rafe." A door on the left side of the long corridor had opened. Red Boltinoff was looking out at him.

"I don't usually get angry about—"

"Better give him that thing," suggested Boltinoff. "Then come on in here."

"I don't like being called—"

"The Fun House just bought a couple of these bouncer andies from the Fresno Enclave," explained Boltinoff. "They're used to working with MexAm pickers."

"So that's supposed to make it—"

"Give me." The big android held out his hand palm up.

"Do you know what this thing is, Red?"

"Yeah, yeah. We'll talk about it. Let the guy have the thing."

"Okay, here." He slapped the Gadget into the andy's hand.

"Thanks, greaseball."

"It's a good thing you don't have a crotch, because if you—"

"This is important, Rafe." Red Boltinoff was a squat freckled man of fifty-two, his nickname deriving from his obviously fictitious hair. He was the boss of the Republic of Southern California News Network.

Rafe was, at the moment, a field reporter for SCNN's Lightside Desk. He shoved by the android and walked into his boss's bordello suite.

Boltinoff had on a plyo lounging robe with a pigeon design. Lying, deathlike, on the big four-poster bed were two plump blonde hooker androids. "I turned off the broads when I heard you out there. Now I know, Rafe, you don't like this sort of place, but when you get to be my age . . . At any rate, I've got to teleport up to the Frisco Enclave in a half hour to attend a Freedom of Speech luncheon. So I had to meet you here if I wanted to tell you the good news."

Rafe leaned against the candy-striped wall, folded his arms. "Good news? You mean something to use on my 'Lightside of the News' broadcasts?"

"No, I mean some good news for you personally." He un-

seamed his robe, shrugged and grunted out of it. "Excuse
me if I suit up while we talk. I think, despite all the dangers
down on the border—"

"Down in what used to be part of Mexico?"

"We won't go into all the technical stuff right this minute,
Rafe. I know that you, because of your MexAm background,
tend to sympathize with the Mexican cause . . . Anyway,
to show you how open-minded SCNN is getting, you've
been promoted."

"Promoted?" Rafe unfolded his arms.

"As of tomorrow, Rafe, you're the new head of the War
Desk." He picked up his all-season undersuit and struggled
into it.

A grin touched Rafe's face. "I've been asking for a move
up for quite a while, but I never expected . . . what's the
War Desk job pay? I know McRobb was getting—"

"You won't be getting quite as much as McRobb . . . to
start. But your salary will increase by $10,000 per year at
once."

"Ten thousand. That's not bad."

Locating his trousers hanging from a bed post, Boltinoff
retrieved them and put them on. "You're not even thirty yet,
Rafe. When I was thirty I was fill-in anchor man on the Ag
Desk out in the San Fernando Sector."

Rafe asked, "Has SCNN changed its position on how we
present the war news?"

"It's going to continue to be 50-50. Fifty per cent of the
Republic's point of view, 50 per cent of the Mexican Territo-
rial Government's."

"And what about Mexx?"

"That's something else I want to talk to you about." He
pulled his shirt on over his head. "SCNN feels we ought to
start including some of the more radical views in our
warcasts. You may never even get a chance to see any of the
Mexx guerrillas, let alone talk to them. If you do, though,
we'll let you put some of what you get on the air."

"Okay, that sounds good," said Rafe. "Suppose you tell me next what that white ball was."

"Nothing we have to worry about. It's NRA's baby."

"So that's a Gadget, huh? I figured."

"Forget it. The problem is National Robot & Android's. You've got the war to worry about, a full-time job." Putting on his jacket, Boltinoff held out his hand. "I've always been very enthusiastic about your work, Rafe. I'm very glad you're on the rise."

As they shook hands Rafe said, "Thanks, Red. I appreciate your—"

"Oh, and don't forget to report to the Medical Wing over at Network Tower in the Movieland Sector."

"What for? I'm not—"

"Everybody who heads into the War Zone has to get an immunity treatment. Not that you're likely to catch anything," said Boltinoff. "By the way, I still have another half hour on these two mechanical bimbos if you'd care to—"

"No, thanks."

The chubby Medic was wearing a 2-piece white doctor-suit. Pinching his pudgy nose between thumb and forefinger, he leaped off the reception room's upper walk ramp to the floor nine feet below.

"See, doesn't that prove you're coocoo?" called one of the white-enameled medical androids who'd been chasing him. White enamel hands on the ramp rail, he squinted down at the fleeing doctor. "You don't see rational everyday physicians taking flying leaps. Right? Admit it."

"Go take a big poop for yourself!" The chubby doctor puffed upright off the thermal hookrug next to the reception desk.

The ball-headed white reception robot glanced over at him. "Really now, Dr. Westchester *cluck*," it said. "Why don't you go along *cluck* quietly."

"Wee wee in your eye." The perspiring physician swung

his head from left to right several times, then dashed toward the door Rafe Santana had just entered by.

Two more of the large-size paramedic andies pushed through the door before he reached it. "We request, Dr. David F. Westchester, that you surrender yourself to us under the provisions of the Goofy Doctor Act."

"Who's goofy? Simply because I cut off a few wrong parts from a few spoilsport patients, does that make me a loony?"

"You're not authorized to cut off *any* parts," the android up on the ramp pointed out. "You're a rectal smear man pure and simple."

"Oh, sure," said Dr. Westchester. "That's a great job for a man with my training. I graduated from the Bible Truth Medical & Faithhealing College of Topeka, Kansas, Heartland Empire, at the head of my class. Now I must spend my days looking into people's poopoos. It's an ignoble and—"

"You're unsettling the people in the *cluck* reception room," the robot warned him.

"I could cure you of that *cluck*, too. What you need is a simple therapeutic amputation. Won't hurt a . . . oof!"

Impatient, the two downstairs androids lunged, each catching him by an arm. One of the andies from upstairs came clanging down and thrust a needle-tipped finger into the struggling Medic's backside.

"You guys are all full of doodoo," he accused, thrashing, attempting to kick them in their metallic groins. "What ought to happen to you is . . . yap!" His mouth snapped shut, his head snapped to the left and he passed suddenly out.

"Oh, I don't like this one bit." The lovely willowy blonde in the neoprene wingchair (next to the one Rafe was thinking of sitting in) pressed her hand against her left breast. "I don't like the notion of their sticking a big sharp needle into that poor goofy man, nor do—"

"Relax, Mona. That's not the kind of shots we're here for,

kiddo." Standing next to her was a lean black man in a nightblue 1-piece cazsuit and knee-length nightblue cape. He was bringing up one of his gloved hands.

"Oh, don't start gesturing at me, Marvo," Mona said, giving an annoyed twist of her lovely shoulders.

Marvo let the hand drop. "Just watch yourself, kid."

"Are you going to Mexico, too, by any chance?" the blonde asked Rafe.

He was watching the stupefied Dr. Westchester being hauled up the ramp. "Yeah," he answered, sitting down finally.

"We're very efficient here in the Medical *cluck* Wing," the robot receptionist said to them. "A doctor does too many wacky things, out he goes *cluck*."

"That's what's going to happen to me surely," Mona said, nodding her head. "A goofy doctor is going to do a wacky thing to me."

"Nix, Mona," advised Marvo. "All we get is a few simple shots and tests. Anybody goes down to entertain the troops goes through this. Don't be antsy, kiddo."

"You're nervous, too. Every time you start using all the strange and bizarre last-century slang I know—"

"Skip it. Everything's going to be swell, kid."

"What kind of act do you have?" Mona asked Rafe.

"I'm a newsman."

"What's it like down there?" the lovely girl wanted to know. "What are my chances of getting mortally wounded in some skirmish?"

"That's not likely," Rafe said, smiling.

"How about the troops? Are they likely to assault me?"

"That I can't tell you."

"Now then," said the receptionist robot. "We'll take Miss Mona Keverne first."

"Oh, yikes."

"Step right up, kiddo. We're rooting for you," said Marvo.

"I'm certain a crazed Medic will . . . oh." She floated up out of her chair, stiffened out until she was parallel to the floor and then went drifting, feet up, for the desk.

"There's a malady you don't often *cluck* see," remarked the robot. "In fact, I don't believe we've ever had a woman who was suffering from levitation in her at—"

"I'm not suffering, he makes me do it."

Marvo had one hand raised high, fingers spread wide. He gave Rafe a shrug and a grin. "I really got telekinetic power," he said. "But for a guy with my ethnic background . . . well, it was easiest to go into show business."

"Put me down, Marvo, and I'll be good," promised Mona.

"Okay, kiddo."

Thump! Krump!

"Too fast," complained Mona, flat out on the floor. "You let me down too fast again."

"There's your trouble with real power," said Marvo. "It's never as dependable as trickery."

The robot instructed, "Right through that door."

A door appeared in a previously blank section of white wall. Mona came to her feet, frowned back at the magician and went out through the fresh opening.

A few moments later Marvo was asked to go through the same door.

And after a few more minutes the mechanical receptionist said, "Now Mr. Rafe Santana *cluck cluck cluck* . . ." With a white-enamel hand he made a flapping gesture at his own back.

Rafe came over to whap it.

"Ah, thank you," said the robot. "If you'll step through the door you see blossoming in yonder wall, everything will be swiftly taken care of."

The door which opened wasn't the same one the others had used. "You sure this is the right way?"

"It is."

The 1st and 2nd Medics were human.

The 2nd was shaking slightly. "Boy, I got the jitters," he said through his neogauze mask.

"Don't drop that thing," cautioned the 1st.

"I'm not that jittery."

"May we proceed?" asked the 3rd Medic, a spotless white surgical robot.

"Sure, okay," said the 2nd. "I shouldn't have stayed so late at that brainstim party last night. That and this new wife I'm trying out are—"

"I'll make the incision," said the surgical robot.

"Sure, you can proceed," said the 1st. He gave the 2nd a gentle nudge. "Don't talk about your private life in front of them."

"Aw, you can trust servos."

Stretched out on the floating operating table, unconscious, was Rafe Santana.

The 1st watched the 3rd cutting into Rafe. "I'd hate to be this guy. That'd be something to give me the jitters."

"He's never going to know anything about it," reminded the 2nd. "He won't even remember this little operation. When he wakes up he'll think he only passed out a couple minutes while taking his tests."

"Yeah, that's true."

"As far as the operation itself goes, there won't be a trace. We do good work here."

"Even so it . . . well, none of our business really."

"He's not going to know a thing about it until . . ."

"It's the until part that unsettles me."

CHAPTER
THREE

The footprints glowed and throbbed on the twilit walkway. "You are walking where the greats have trod," the nearest tiny gutter-speaker informed Rafe.

"Yeah, I know." Each set of footprints was sunk in a rectangle of syncrete and outlined with a pulsing length of light-tubing. The row of famous footprints stretching out ahead of him seemed blurry.

"You've just stepped," informed the next gutter-speaker, "into the footsteps of Rance Keane, noted gunfighter, who is by apt coincidence, now appearing—"

"This isn't Rance Keane's square. It says Butch the Wonder Dog."

"You sure?" asked the tiny speaker. "It's supposed to be—"

"Unless Rance Keane has four furry feet, this is Butch."

"Well, sir, be that as it may, Rance Keane is appearing only blocks from this very spot at the 11th Annual West States Shoot Out Concert and—"

"I'm groggier than I realized," said Rafe, "standing around talking to the sidewalk." He hopped off the walkway, trotted over to the pedramp which would take him to La Cienega Blvd. and the MexAm restaurant he'd decided to have dinner in.

He had the feeling he'd been unconscious longer than they'd told him. But his watch and the Medical Wing clocks didn't back that up.

"Why'd I pass out from a simple blood test anyway?"

Bam! Wam! Bam!

A huge inflated neorub effigy of Rance Keane was rising up over the gunfight stadium, giant 6-guns spinning and firing in its enormous fists.

Scratching at the back of his neck, Rafe stopped and, absently, watched the illuminated gunfighter bobbing in the thickening dusk. "Did something happen besides those routine tests and shots? Yeah, but what could—"

Ching! Ching! Wap!

"One side, brother, or we'll knock you on your fundament, kind sir."

Seven seminarians in tinted see-through robes were coming along the pedway, shaking electric tambourines and battery-operated prayer-wheels. Three girls and four men, all seedy and disarrayed.

It was a girl who'd requested Rafe to make way. A very slender, but large-breasted, blonde with a tambourine in each hand.

The seminarian immediately behind her carried a round white ball, ten-knobbed, in his left hand. "We're making a pilgrimage, dearly beloved, so you'd best haul arse out of our way."

Rafe, grinning, stepped to the edge of the walkway.

"Sure, and bless you all," he said. "What denomination are you?"

"We're from the Venice Beach Retreat," answered the unkempt blonde, "if it's any of your humping business, sweet friend."

"Got a Gadget, huh?" Rafe asked.

"Watch out," warned one of the young men, "this chuzzler might be a cop."

"Naw, he's no cop," said the blonde girl. "Come on, we've got to job the gate 'bots and get into the auditorium right now if we don't want to miss Rance Keane."

Rafe watched the string of see-through-robed seminarians parade by. Then he continued, slowly, on his way.

He'd gone a block farther when he heard the hum of stunguns from up ahead. Behind him at the same time commenced the hissing of wheels. Three rollcops came whizzing by him going toward the gunfight auditorium. Each of the robot cops was cylindrical, multi-armed and mounted on two cycle-type wheels.

"Crashers, crashers, crashers," one of the mechanical cops was bleating.

Rafe decided to follow them.

Another trio of rollcops was approaching the ticket area from another walkway, fitting stunrods and wapstiks into their various hands.

Bam! Wam! Bam!

The Rance Keane effigy, up there in the new darkness a hundred feet above the forming struggle, was firing away.

"Get that scrapping thing to work, Brother Jocko!"

"Trying, Sister Mercy." The seminarian with the Gadget was shaking it, punching at its knobs.

A human gatecop was taking swings at them with his stunrod. "Try to sneak in, will you? For shame. And you people of the cloth."

"You nerf, Brother Jocko!" accused the blonde, see-through robe flapping as she dodged the wooshing swing of a stunrod. "You didn't follow the plan right!"

"I did, too!"

"Then how come it didn't work on the ticket 'bots?"

"Worked on the skybus, didn't it? Worked at the Welcaf, didn't it? Worked—"

Slam!

The gatecop's stunrod got Brother Jocko. He stiffened, arms going wide.

There were a half dozen rollcops circling the seminarians. On their first charge the robot police used only their wapstiks. The two-foot long plastic sticks flashed and sang like whips, slapping the seminarians.

The blonde girl stumbled, fell to one knee. Two cops rolled in on her, both worrying her with wapstiks, repeating and repeating, "Crashers, crashers, crashers!"

"Get the damn kid with the Gadget," yelled the gatecop.

Rafe was running. He hit into one of the rollcops with his shoulder, reached down to give the blonde girl a hand up. "Get away from her," he shouted. "You guys know you're not supposed to—"

Wap!

Incredible circles of pain began radiating through Rafe's body from the point where the rollcop's wapstik had hit him. His fingers pronged, he let go the fallen girl. The pain was so intense it made him huddle in on himself, teeth grinding, tears splashing out of his eyes. *"Dios!"*

He smelled something then, a harsh medicinal smell. A vision of an absolutely white room rushed across his mind.

At the same time he was rolling up his right sleeve. "Press," he managed to say.

The gatecop recognized the newsman ID tape around Rafe's wrist. "Back off, boys," he urged the rollcops. "This boy is media." He ceased pummeling the seminarians. "Best we call a halt to this incident."

"Bad press, bad press," muttered several of the robots. "Avoid, avoid."

The swinging arms slowed, stopped, flapped down. The robots rolled back.

Some of the pain was diminishing. After gulping in a breath, Rafe told the seminarians, "Get away from here, and hide that damn Gadget."

Five of them, dragging the stunned Brother Jocko, went scurrying off at once.

The blonde girl got up, rubbing at the dark spots on her arms and legs. "Thanks, brother," she said to Rafe.

"We don't want the spotlight of publicity thrown on us," the gatecop said. "Even though I think one of those kids had one of those dinguses."

Rafe nodded at him, pushed through the ring of hesitant rollcops. The pain across his back continued to fade.

And with the pain went the memory he'd been trying to catch hold of.

CHAPTER
FOUR

Bong!

"Chuckleheads!" cried the very old man as they carried him into the subterranean meeting room. "You banged my nincompoop leg into the wall and—"

Wang! Bung!

"There, you did it again. You chumps."

Both the broad-shouldered headless robots made apologetic whirrings inside their tank-shaped bodies.

"No wonder the entire loony world is taking advantage of National Rob . . . oof."

One of the white-enameled robots had thrust a thermometer into the old man's wrinkle-ringed mouth. "Health test," it said out of the talkhole in its midsection.

Spitting angrily, old Nelson Hackensacker, Jr., got the

plastic stick out. "What a pair of ninnyhammers," he screamed. "Burton, is this the best we can do in the way of med 'bots?"

Gil Burton was a dark chubby man seated at one side of the floating oval conference table. "We made these particular 'bots 12 per cent oversolicitous, sir, to assure—"

"Chowderhead," said the Chairman of the Board of National Robot & Android. "These tomtugs are 25 per cent too fawning at least. And that tastes like a rectal thermometer you used on me."

"Aiee, sahib," groaned the medical robot, "a thousand pardons. Wrong orifice. May the whips of your scorn chastise the backside of my—"

"Who programmed them to talk like a couple of nancy wogs?"

"Ahum." Burton fiddled with the chart-projector in front of him.

Directly across the table was Cardinal Newfound of the Gay Pentecostal Church. "Oh, don't mind me, sweetie," he said.

"Get me sat down," Hackensacker, Jr., ordered his attending robots.

They carried him to the head of the floating table, placed him in the complex life-support chair and proceeded to hook him up.

"The country was in bad enough shape when it was run by that goosecap Sturdy himself," said the old man. "Now he's got this painted prettywilly advising him." He shook his head in disgust, causing three of his life-support wires to detach from his neck.

"I think, lovey, it was just awfully brave of Sturdy to come out of the closet," said Cardinal Newfound, rubbing a handful of jeweled rings on the front of his scarlet robe. "Simply because I'm the gray eminence behind the presidential throne, dearie, doesn't mean—"

"Be still," suggested Hackensacker. "The president of the

new United Federation is a fruitcake, okay. His Secretary of State is a fruitcake, okay. I accept those facts, but don't go pushing your—"

"Might I remind you, honeybunch," said the cardinal, "that I'm President Sturdy's official rep at this little chitchat today. If you have any hope of the United States ever getting completely back on its feet again, you'd darned well better treat—"

"The United States, fragmented as it is, is enough on its feet to have provided NRA with a gross profit of $39,000,000 last year," cut in the old man. "If it wasn't for those nincompoop Gadgets, we'd have taken in at least $6,000,000 more. Too many people are getting free use of our mechs, cheating us out of our per cent of all our clients' take. Which is why—"

"Okay you, right in there!"

Turkey, the bedraggled thief, came staggering into the conference room. "Easy with your scrapping mitts," he said over his shoulder to the stocky man who'd shoved him in.

"Right in our backyard," said Arnold Bennish, the Head Troubleshooter for NRA. "That's what things are coming to."

Turkey fell over his mismatched boots, went tumbling over onto the thermal rug. "I don't believe any of this is strictly legal."

"Allow me to help you, honey." Cardinal Newfound, scarlet robes fluttering, rose to aid the fallen thief.

"What is this guy, some kind of wisp?" Turkey, upright again, addressed himself to the ancient chairman of NRA.

"Who," Hackensacker asked of Bennish, "is this muggins?"

"Quit squawking. I'll explain." Bennish took a Gadget out of his pocket and tossed it at the old man.

Bong! Clong!

Both robots tried to catch it, colliding.

Hackensacker snatched it away. "A new variation," he said after squinting at the white knobby sphere.

"Every time we build in an anti-Gadget defense," said Burton, "they come up with a modification of the Gadget."

"I caught this guy over at the Country Club Hospital," Bennish told them. "Yeah, the Country Club Hospital. He was blissfully making use of all the facilities."

"This can't be legal, can it?" said Turkey. "Dragging me into some wisp den and maltreating me and—"

"It's a federal crime to use a Gadget."

Turkey laughed. "Don't try to scrap me. There is no federal government. Hasn't been since around—"

"The United Federation was formed in 2013, you young ninny. At the moment nearly 75 per cent of—"

"No scrap? Never heard a word about that down in the Westport Shanty Town. Interesting."

"Sit down," Bennish said. "There."

Eying the indicated chair, Turkey said, "Don't I get to call the Law Bank?"

"Sit."

Turkey sat. "I still get the distinct feeling my civil liberties are being trampled."

Bennish walked toward the chair. "Who's Crackpot?"

"Who?"

"Crackpot!"

"Never heard the name."

"He invented the Gadget."

"No scrap? That's news to me, but then I didn't even know we had a United States again." He glanced at the cardinal. "Those are handsome earrings, your grace. I mooged a similar pair once from a—"

"Why exactly did you drag this loony in here, Bennish? To illustrate how unsuccessful you've been in wiping out the Gadget?"

"To make you realize, you old fart, the problem is a hell of a lot more serious than your decayed old brain will admit," Bennish told him. "This guy is a living symbol of how things are. Using a Gadget practically on the NRA

grounds. There I was having a routine brainwave test and I
see this piece of garbage ordering—"

"That's another violation of my basic rights, isn't it? First
you kidnap me, boot me in the cannister, drag me here and
start using offensive lang—"

"I want more men on my staff," Bennish said to Hackensacker. "I want a bigger budget."

"We," said Burton, "upped your budget only five weeks
ago, Arnie."

"Do you want me to follow up on the new lead I've got or
not?"

"Who is this Crackpot?" Turkey asked the cardinal in a
low voice.

"No one you need worry about, lovey. You really like the
earrings, do you? Would you—"

"Am I late for the torture? Gee, I hope not." A slim
twenty-two-year-old boy in a tweed jumpsuit came hurrying
in. It was Howie Peet, Director of the United Federation Secret Police. "Is that the subject? He looks like he'll break before we even get started."

"Torture?" Turkey sat up straight. "You can't torture me,
can you? That's worse than kidnapping. There must be a
law against torture, isn't there?"

"Well, Hackensacker, do I get the money or not?"

"Yes, yes. Now take this cabbagehead out of here."

"Don't we get to torture him?" Peet seated himself on the
other side of Cardinal Newfound. "Boy, I really do think
torture's one of the greatest law-enforcement tools we've
got."

Burton was watching the troubleshooter. "Do you really
have a new and positive lead on Crackpot? As to who he is
and where he is?"

"Yeah, but it's going to cost us. I'm going to have to buy
information."

"Isn't that what you've been doing?"

"This is a different setup." Bennish jabbed a finger into Turkey's side. "You sure you never heard of Crackpot?"

"Jabbing a guy in the ribs can't be legal either."

"Get him out of here," said old Hackensacker. "You've made your point and the odor of this young dunderhead is starting to—"

"I was going to take a steam bath when—"

"Carry this bastard down to a holding room," Bennish told one of the medical robots.

"Shall I, sahib?" the robot asked the old man.

"Use the Gadget," suggested Turkey, "and they have to do whatever you want."

CHAPTER FIVE

Down below him in the bright morning huge rooftop words glowed.

Fun!
Girls!
Sport!

A blabmissile came circling around Rafe's robotcruiser, its six horn-shaped speakers announcing, "Welcome to Tijuana, California, *amigo!* This is the place to have some fun! Welcome to Tijuana, California, *amigo!* This is the place to have some fun! Welcome to . . ."

With an angry growl Rafe switched on the dash TV, turning the sound up high.

". . . better standard of living to the peons," one of the tiny men on the oval screen was saying.

"Horsepuckey!" broke in the thick-set bearded man next to him on the long lime-green floating sofa. "All we're doing for the Mexican peons is killing them off. Now, Bruce, I've covered a hell of a lot of wars and this—"

"Edgar Allan Boskow." Rafe recognized the feisty RSCNN war correspondent.

A fragile blond man at the sofa end, after coughing, said, "We'll return to this stimulating debate on the moral validity of our position in this conflict with Mexico when 'Aspects of War' returns in three minutes."

A naked girl, decorated with cosmetic polka dots and gold bangles, replaced the debaters on the screen. "How'd you like to spend a night with a hot ticket like me?" she inquired in a husky voice. "I bet I'm every man's idea of a terrific lay. Yet not so long ago I was merely another frustrated housefrau. Then I heard about the International Home Hooker School of—"

Rafe got rid of her image.

A second later his cruiser began to drop.

"Hey, we're not landing till Guaymas," he told the robot control panel.

The ship continued to fall.

With a lurching grab Rafe got hold of the manual controls, tried to get back the cruiser from the robot mechanisms. The control rods were frozen.

"Welcome to Tijuana, California, *amigo!* This is the place to have some fun!" The blabmissile was following him down.

"I don't want to have any damn fun," Rafe said. "If this is some kind of Chamber of Commerce stunt to—"

Thunk! Thud!

His robotcruiser had landed on a high Tijuana rooftop.

Rafe tugged at the manual control rods.

Something tapped on the cabin's neoglass dome.

Turning, he saw a hairy hand clutching a white knobby ball.

"Going my way?" inquired the bearded man who stood out there in the midmorning glare.

"Edgar Allan Boskow." Rafe opened the cabin door. "I thought you were debating the morality of war with Bruce Dingdarling."

"That bullpuckey was taped last week."

"Moral situations can change in a week. How'd you get my ship down?"

"With this little bugger." The war correspondent held up his Gadget.

"It's good for that, too?"

"With one of these you can control just about any servomech known to man, Rafael. Which is why NRA is puckeying in its drawers over them."

"Where you heading?"

"Guaymas, same as you. When I heard you were due this way about this time I climbed up here to flag myself a lift," explained Boskow. "Did you know we're atop the best bordello in Annexed Mexico. All human staff."

"You couldn't tell from the roof."

"If you're the best, you can afford to be subtle. No glow-signs, no blabbers." Grunting, he pulled himself up into the cabin. "You I had no trouble spotting. Our esteemed network has RSCNN smeared all over this cruiser."

As soon as Boskow was strapped into the passenger seat Rafe nudged the ascend button. The robot was working for him once again. They went straight up for three hundred feet and then shot off in the direction of Guaymas. "Buy your Gadget in Mexico?"

"You mean Annexed Mexico." The bearded correspondent dropped the Gadget into a jacket pocket. "Your homeland is part of the Republic now. If you're going to cover the war for RSCNN, Rafael, you'll have to remember that."

"Good thing I picked you up, Ed. You can fill me in on all the moral issues."

"Horsepuckey. I'm not any fonder of what the Republic is doing down here than you are," said Boskow. "But a newsman, and I don't mean a kissfanny like Bruce Dingdarling . . . a real newsman *reports*. He strives to get the truth to the people. Taking sides, though, can screw you up."

"Being truthful and nonpartisan," said Rafe, "is a tough job."

"I've done it down here for two years. Before that, if you remember my reporting of the Brazil war, Rafael, you know—"

"Yeah, I know. Where'd you buy the Gadget?"

"Didn't buy it. Made it from a plan I bought in Hermosillo. This Crackpot guy is a real genius, Rafael, because the Gadget can control an infinity of robots, androids, servos. Yet it's as simple as—"

"Who's Crackpot?"

"Rafael, you've been looking at the light side too long. You've never heard of Crackpot?"

"Nope. Who is he?"

Boskow chuckled. "Ah, National Robot & Android would give untold and unspecified amounts of wealth to learn that," he said. "Crackpot is the alleged inventor of the Gadget. His identity continues to remain a secret."

Nodding, Rafe looked out over the annexed countryside. Yellow fields were unrolling. "Hasn't been any fighting here."

"Not yet."

"I've wanted to cover this war for a long time, Ed," said Rafe. "Now I'm here, though, I'm wondering if I can do things the way I want without getting stepped on by RSCNN."

"You're going to do a terrific job," Boskow assured him.

CHAPTER SIX

The transparent corridor curled and twisted along the water's edge. It was faintly tinted, making the Gulf of California a deeper blue and giving the bright afternoon sand a licorice hue. Rafe, his two suitcases following him on a robot-dolly, was walking along the snaking corridor toward the suite of his new boss.

The ghost of the suite's old name still showed on the door, *Bridal Chamber*, above the new designation, *Regional News Chief*.

Rafe halted and knocked on the door.

The dolly kept on rolling, ran between his legs and hit the door. The door swung inward.

"What did they do, send me an eager one?" Clifford Less

was sitting in a body shape-chair next to an enormous vibrabed.

"Not me," Rafe said into the big room, "the luggage cart."

The robot-dolly was circling the room, banging into computers, mirrored walls and packing crates. Rafe's suitcases fell off just as the cart dropped into the sunken bathing area.

"Sit in that chair over there, Santana," the News Chief said, pointing at a pink floating chair. He was a thin, pale, weary-looking man of fifty. "Don't press any of its buttons or it'll hug you and massage your private parts. Left over from when this was the newlywed suite. Though why you'd want a chair to diddle you when you had a broad . . . Have a pleasant trip down?"

Rafe seated himself carefully in the pink chair. It made a tentative grab at his backside and then subsided. "Yep. I stopped to give a ride to Ed Boskow."

Wrinkles formed on Less' forehead. "You are chummy with the fabled Edgar Allan Boskow?"

"Know him," replied Rafe. "I admire some of what he's done, his casts from the field."

"Heartwarming, huh?" Less reached out and began feeling the top of the bed, which was strewn with faxmemos, voicegram printouts, hand-scribbled notes, talkspools, vidsics. "First off I'd better—"

Gurgle! Spurgle!

"I think your luggage cart is taking a bath."

Rafe crossed to peer into the bath pit. "Can't tell, there's too much steam."

"Kick that red knob, it'll turn the works off."

Doing that, Rafe returned to his chair. "When do you want me to take over the War Desk?"

"You can do the six-o'clock cast tonight," Less told him. "You've seen McRobb anchor the War Desk, haven't you?"

"Watch him most nights. I have an interest in this particular war."

"We'll go into that in a minute." He'd located the memo he was seeking. "Let me read you a recent pronouncement from the Republic's Secretary of the Press. Ahum . . . 'Maybe our morals are not perfect but they are better than others. Republic of Southern California policy and, yes, United Federation policy, too, is regarded through what's left of the world as a pillar of freedom. This is a thought you must keep in mind while presenting the news of our unfortunate conflict with Mexico to the public. You must emphasize, though deftly, that the Republic position is the right moral one. Minimize, while not totally ignoring, the Mexican claims that our motives in annexing are based on a desire for commercial gains and new territory to exploit. Emphasize, rather, the fact we are bringing a stability to the Mexican people, giving them a security which they haven't ever had under the fluctuating regimes in Mexico City.'" Less let that memo drop to the vibrabed, gazed up at the mirrored ceiling and then selected another piece of fax-paper. "This came in two days ago from the Secretary. Hum . . . '. . . nothing basically wrong with having a MexAm anchor the War Desk. Indeed it may, subtly of course, serve to emphasize that the Mexican people do accept and comprehend what we are doing for them.' Isn't that nice?"

Rafe's hands had tightened to fists. He cleared his throat. "I want this job," he said. "So read me everything Secretary McRaine has to say."

"Only this one more, fresh off the voxbox this morning. Aham . . . '. . . do not believe Mexx represents the thoughts and feelings of the people. While we, too, oppose the current President of Mexico, we do not share the guerrilla point of view, let us be sure to emphasize, that he is a ruthless dictator. We can foresee, once the Republic and Mexico have reached the conference table, a long period of stable and friendly relationships between Annexed Mexico and the remainder of Mexico. However, in the interest of freedom of the press, something which we continually em-

phasize we are in favor of, and in light of the presence of a
gifted MexAm anchor man on the RSCNN War Desk from
hence on, it will be to everyone's advantage to allow for
some presentation of the Mexx view.' Unquote and amen."

Rafe sat watching his new boss. "I sense, and let me
emphasize this, you don't quite believe much of what the
Secretary of the Press has to say."

"Did you gather that impression from the way I read his
manifestos?" Less' eyebrows rose, causing many new wrinkles to show up on his gaunt face. "Must be my inflections.
There's the reason I never did well on camera. I used to
read these heart-tugging items about soldiers in Brazil help-
ing little native kids raise puppy dogs after they'd burned
down their town for them, and I got a terrible reputation for
being a cynic. The day I broadcast the story about how thir-
teen commandos bought a new bell for the San Norberto
church I . . . suffice it to say I came West and convinced
RSCNN I'd reformed. I also agreed not to appear on a telecast anymore. Just as well, since a skinny newsman tends to
unsettle people. You've got to be either handsome or
pudgy."

Rafe said, "So I'm not really going to be able to report on
the Mexx guerrillas' side of things?"

"Oh, you'll be allowed." Less drummed his fingers on the
ornate bedspread. "Don't know for how long. Did you say
you were a friend of Boskow's?"

"I don't dislike the guy," Rafe answered. "Actually, I
don't have any close friends."

"A loner, huh? That's what they used to say about me.
Now they don't even bother to talk about me behind my
back much."

Rafe asked, "McRobb made it up to the fight zone fairly
often. Am I going to be stuck here in Guaymas, or do I get
up there, too?"

"This week we, or rather they, want you to stick here. Get
used to the setup, get the feel of anchoring the War Desk.

You have to write all your own linking copy for your cast. You've got a half hour of air time. With all our taped stuff you usually have six to eight minutes of tying together and analyzing to do."

"I wrote all my own copy for the 'Lightside' cast."

Less made a chuckling noise. "No light side down here, Santana," he said.

CHAPTER SEVEN

The houseboat restaurant bobbed gently on the black water. The proprietor leaned close to Rafe to say, "I wouldn't order the seafood plate."

Rafe said, "Not going to order anything until my friend arrives."

The proprietor was a big wide man, dressed in a two-piece off-white evening suit. "They're dumping some kind of leftover chemical weapon stuff in the gulf," he explained in a low voice, glancing at the dozen or so other customers scattered around the softly swaying room. "The fish tastes okay, but for six or eight hours after you eat it you have an uncontrollable urge to tell the truth. I confide this in you, because in your business—"

"I appreciate that."

The proprietor sat opposite Rafe. "I'm in the communications business, too, on the side. The way I get scrapped by my publisher I can't make a full-time living at it. I'm an author."

"Oh, so?"

"You've probably never heard of me. My name is Fulmer Anderson."

"I haven't."

"My trouble, besides a publisher who's snarfing me, is I keep creating immortal characters. You do that and readers won't know you, they'll only know your immortal characters. I wager you can't tell me who wrote Sherlock Holmes, Tarzan or Fu Manchu."

"Conan Doyle, Edgar Rice Burroughs and Sax Rohmer. What immortal characters have you created?"

"Well, someone with a literary background such as you obviously have possibly doesn't read series books," said Fulmer Anderson. "I write the Masochist series and the Sadist series, and my latest series is about Mr. & Mrs. Lust."

"I'm not, you're right, as familiar with them as I am with Sherlock Holmes."

"My objective is not to change the world, although a world where publishers don't moog your earnings and the army doesn't dump things in the water would suit me better. I am purely and simply an entertainer," he explained. "In the Sadist series I'm trying to give a few hours of adventurous entertainment to my readers. The basic premise of my Sadist series is that the hero goes around to exciting places and hurts people. He hurts about six people per book. Now the Masochist is different. He travels to the romantic, adventurous places of the world and people hurt him. My plots are not first-rate, but I have a lush style which—"

"Anderson, I read your newest Mr. & Mrs. Lust book and I found it loathsome and disgusting." Edgar Allan Boskow had come stomping up to the table. He grabbed the back of the proprietor's chair and yanked it back.

"Why, thanks, Edgar. That's exactly the effect I was striving for," said Anderson. "Some readers tend to miss the point, so I'm glad you—"

"Bring us a couple of bottles of Bombilla Beer." Boskow urged Anderson out of the chair, then put himself in it. "Caught your cast tonight, Rafael. Damn good."

"I think I came across pretty subdued."

"Naw, you had a real dynamic quality, just right."

"Here are your beers." Anderson placed two glasses and two frosted bottles atop the table. "I won't linger around to—"

"Damn right you won't. Go away and crank out one of those vile and perverted books of yours."

"Can we possibly quote you on a jacket blurb, Edgar. 'Vile and perverted,' says noted war correspond—"

"Away, go away," insisted Boskow. "You can't let people soak up your time, Rafael. You'll find down here in Annexed Mexico nearly everybody's got something to tell or something to sell."

"Some of it might turn out to be news."

"Naw, Rafael, I can tell you all the news you need to know."

Rafe poured his beer into his plexglass. "Okay, how about Mexx? Less tells me I can devote more time to the guerrilla side of the war. How can I contact somebody who—"

"Let them contact you," advised Boskow. "Two King-United men have disappeared so far trying to see Carregador, also some dimwit girl from *Newz* magazine."

"I don't have to talk to the head guy," said Rafe. "If Carregador is too tough to get at, I'll settle for one of his lieutenants. Eventually, though, I'd—"

"Concentrate on the War Desk for the nonce," Boskow said before guzzling his beer straight from the bottle. Wiping foam from his beard, he added, "If, in a couple weeks, you still want to get close to a Mexx spokesman, I'll see what I can do."

"You've got contacts?"

"I've got contacts with everybody."

Rafe sat back and concentrated on drinking his beer. They talked of other things than the guerrillas for a half hour. Then Rafe stood. "Going to the john." He went walking across the tilting floor.

The men's room was dim, smelling strongly of a floral-based disinfectant. A woebegone android attendant in a threadbare buff-color worksuit stood next to the wash basin with a dry-nozzle clutched in one hand.

"*Buenas noches*, sir," it croaked.

Rafe, returning the greeting, headed toward a stall.

"Hey, I got a message for you, Rafe," said the attendant. "Not much time to give it to you, so pay good attention."

Rafe came closer to the machine. "You're not an andy."

"No, this is a disguise."

"Then who—"

"Listen, *amigo*. Mexx wants to talk to you."

"I want to talk to them, so how—"

"Be at the Church of St. Isaac at four o'clock tomorrow afternoon. Don't tell nobody about this, don't let nobody follow you."

"I'll be there. How'll I know your agent?"

"She knows you."

Rafe frowned. "It's someone I know?"

"That's all I can tell you for now." He looked toward the door, dropped the dry-nozzle and pushed out of the washroom.

"She?" Rafe said to himself.

Edgar Allan Boskow guided his landcar swiftly through the late-night streets of the MexAm section of Guaymas, using the barkmike to warn the live hookers and hustlers out of his way.

"Trash," he said. "I used to think wars brought it out."

The landcar shot up a ramp and into a parking platform

above a twenty-four-hour cantina named the Vista De Pajaro.

When he was alone in the customer elevator, the bearded correspondent thrust a special key into a slot on the control panel. The elevator let him out at a special floor.

Boskow tromped along a cool, gray corridor and went into a cool, gray room.

Three men sat in the room, only one of them in uniform, around a floating neowood table.

Boskow stopped in front of the table. "They've contacted him," he reported. "He's going to see the girl tomorrow afternoon."

CHAPTER EIGHT

Half past three and the belltapes in the tower of St. Isaac Church began to toll. Rafe could see the tower from the cobbled street he was walking along, see a few doves go swinging up into the bright clear afternoon. He'd left his quarters at the network resort a little before three and he was certain no one had followed him. He didn't intend to talk about his meeting until after it had happened. Not to Less, not to Boskow.

The gradually climbing street was quiet, striped with afternoon shade. Rafe turned a corner and walked into noise and people.

A huge skyvan was dropping down toward a landing, belching multicolor balloons out of its underside. Emblazoned all over the van were the words IT'S TIME FOR MR. GIG-GLE!

"Hey, kids! What time is it?" roared the speakers mounted in the skyvan's belly. "That's right! It's time for Mr. Giggle . . . and Knuckles!"

Out of a large white building encrusted with wrought iron a young woman in the one-piece black jumpsuit of a hospital nun came running. "*Por favor,*" she called toward the descending craft. "Some of our little ones can't be subjected to such noise."

Boom! Boom! Boom!

Three cannons on the van's roof began shooting out colored smoke and confetti.

"We're here to cheer up all you little patients," promised the speakers. "Let's sing the Mr. Giggle song!"

"No, please, no singing." The nun was pounding, cautiously, on the van door. "The explosions are bad enough. We appreciate your coming to entertain our little patients, but—"

"Singing and laughter never hurt anyone, ma'am." Mr. Giggle emerged from the skyvan as it settled down in the middle of the narrow street. "Why many's the ailing tot I've seen throw away his—"

"A good many of our patients, as you know, are war casualties, señor. We—"

"What's her ferking problem?" A tiny silver-plated man came bounding out of the van.

Mr. Giggle, who was large and pink in a polka-dot poncho, made a grab for the little android. "Okay, who's the wiseass who programmed Knuckles to be blue?" he asked into the van.

Several of his musicians chortled as they disembarked.

"Stuff it in your nerf," taunted Knuckles, jigging on the curb in front of the children's hospital.

"We appreciate your efforts to help our morale, señor,"

the young nun said to Rafe, who'd stopped for a moment to watch the hullabaloo. "Could you, however—"

"I'm not part of this troop," Rafe said. "But I'll quiet them down."

He pushed through the unloading musicians, approached the clanking Knuckles. With one swing of his right arm he caught up the robot-dummy. Rafe had worked with similar mechanisms on some of his "Lightside" shows, so he knew how to work the backside control panel.

"Hey, greaseball, what's the idea futzing with my bott," exclaimed Knuckles. "You can . . . Golly, I sure have been acting silly, ain't I? Saying bad words and all. Gosh, Mr. Giggle, what'll the boys and girls think of me?"

Rafe tossed the little mechanical man to polka-dotted Mr. Giggle. "Less noise," he suggested.

"Who the hell do you think you are?" Mr. Giggle shouted at him. "Maybe you peons aren't familiar with the way things are up in the Republic. 'Mr. Giggle & Knuckles' is the top-ranked kid show in the West States. We're doing you a hell of a favor coming down here to put on free shows. Walt Reisberson, writing in the *Greater LA Times-Exam*, characterized our show as 'a sheer delight, a sizzling production. I sat glued to my . . .' Oof!"

Rafe had prodded Mr. Giggle in his ample stomach. "I don't have time for your whole crew of idiots, Giggle, but I can take a few moments for you," he said. "So if you'd—"

"No, no." Mr. Giggle, after looking into Rafe's angry face, backed off, Knuckles tucked up tight in his armpit. "We'll tred lightly and quietly." To the milling musicians he said, "Let's keep it down, fellas."

Rafe moved on.

The holy water font needed adjusting. It was spewing water up in a thin stream which hit the pseudomarble ceiling of the foyer of the St. Isaac Church. The salty water splashed the walls, puddled on the pseudomarble floor.

A robot priest, one of the old-style black cylinder types, was flat on his back beside the font. Apparently he'd slipped on the slick flooring and been unable to upright himself. He was sprawled there, wheels spinning futilely, muttering, "*Mea culpa, mea culpa, mea culpa, mea culpa.*"

"Let me help you, padre." Rafe stooped, got a hand under one of the robot priest's several arms.

"Bless you, my son," spoke the robot when he was back on his wheels. He made a lopsided sign of the cross with one of his arms. "Have you come to see the magnificent Church of St. Isaac? It is one of the finest completely mechanized churches of God in the entire Western world."

Rafe was looking through the glass doors of the church proper. There was only one person in the long, domed church. Far up, close to the neon-trimmed altar a girl was kneeling in a coin-operated pew. "I would like simply to pray, padre."

"So be it, my son," said the priest out of his midsection voicehole. "If you could roll me clear of these slippery stretches I'll go fetch the sexton-servo to clean up this mess."

Rafe guided the robot across the foyer to an exit. Then he entered the church. The girl was slim, dark-haired. He didn't think he recognized her.

And yet, as he got closer, there was something . . .

"Susan!"

Two of the robot saints cautioned, "Hush!" from their neon-lit alcoves. St. Joseph added, "No yelling in the house of the Lord!"

It was Susan Cereza. She was standing, facing him. "Hello, Rafe," she said softly.

He became aware of his breathing, felt an odd tingling across his chest. He stopped beside her. "Six years," he said.

"Nearer seven," Susan answered. She was very pretty, with high cheekbones and dark, glowing eyes. "Sit beside me so we can talk."

He found a coin, dropped it into the coinbox. "You're with Mexx?" He moved into the pew, sat on the bench close to the slender girl.

"For over three years." She was studying him. "I'm a little surprised you came today at all."

"Why? We were . . . what? Friends . . . no, more than friends."

"We were in love," the girl said. "That was in college, in a different country and a long time ago. I wasn't surprised that you ignored my other tries at contacting you."

"What other tries?"

"I wrote to you three times in the past year, at your home in the Santa Monica Sector. You never answered, but—"

"I never got any letters from you, Susan. Not one. I didn't know where you were, not after you left Greater Los Angeles."

"And you stayed." She shrugged gently. "It's no matter. Maybe getting this close to the war has changed—"

"Damn it," he said loudly, taking hold of her hand, "I tell you, Susan, I never got one letter from you!"

"Hush!" called out two saints and the Virgin Mary.

"Perhaps not. I thought, when we learned you were coming here to Mexico, it would be worth one more try." She moved her hand out of his.

"You're speaking for Mexx, not for yourself?"

"For the guerrilla army, yes," Susan told him. "You decided to stay in the Republic and rise inside their setup. I decided to come back to Mexico. That was the end of it, seven years ago."

"Now that you want a favor, though, you figure—"

"You can look at it that way if you want, Rafe," she said. "You have an important position with the news network. Mexx wants to get its side of things to more people. Not that we think it will solve our problems. No, the final change for Mexico will be a military one. But Carregador believes the more people who know what we really stand for, the easier and sooner will be our victory."

"You're fighting against both sides," he said.

"Mexx wants your Republic of Southern California out of Mexico, wants the annexed territory returned," the girl said. "Even after that happens there is still President Zurrapa in Mexico City. Now, as you must know even from the biased reports which come across your War Desk, we are concentrating on getting rid of the Republic Army as quickly as possible. We do not fight side by side with the government forces, however."

"Might be better if you did. Two armies against one is better odds."

"If Zurrapa could be trusted. He is even less rational than your Republic generals. President Zurrapa would risk his own defeat to destroy Carregador and the Mexx forces. The few early attempts we made to co-operate ended with our people being betrayed and killed."

Rafe leaned back, watching the giant crucifix over the altar flash off and on. "Okay," he said finally, "my network tells me I can give air time to Mexx. Can you set up an interview with Carregador?"

"Yes, he's anxious to do that. Shortly, and even I don't know where as yet, there will be a meeting between Carregador and some of the other Mexx leaders. You, only you alone, can attend. You are to bring no one with you."

"I'll work with a robot cameraman."

"Obviously, we'll make very careful plans for taking you to Carregador," Susan said. "When the details are worked out, you'll be contacted again." She stood up.

"Listen, Susan, I really never did get any messages or—"

"Yes, probably not." She moved away from him, toward the opposite aisle. "*Adios*, Rafael."

Rafe remained where he was, watching the slim girl leave by way of a shadowy side door. "She looks exactly the way she did back . . ." He shook his head, left the pew and walked up the main aisle of the Church of St. Isaac. "Too long ago."

The robot priest had fallen down again out in the foyer.

Rafe stepped over him and went out into the late afternoon.

CHAPTER NINE

The wheelchair, of his own design, carried the fat young man across the thick Oriental carpets of the silent underground room. His name was Lewis Arundel, he was twenty-six and had been complexly crippled since an accident which had befallen him shortly after his fourth birthday. The accident had taken place a quarter of a mile from here, up above in one of the processing plants. The factory was still there, but completely redesigned. Lewis had seen to that, years ago.

His gleaming silver-plated chair stopped before a low table. "Come on, come on," Lewis said in his high-pitched voice. "Let's see a little more damn efficiency."

A metallic arm at the side of the table swung out, picked up a packet of Arundel Soysnax and dropped it on his lap.

Then an arm of the wheelchair picked up the packet, held it so Lewis' good hand could yank the ripcord. The fat young man scrooped his thick pale fingers into the packet, grabbing out diamond-shape soychips and jamming them into his mouth. "Hold that scrapping bag up higher," he told the chair, mouth thick with chunks of chips.

The chair did.

"Lot 2000-00-XT7, huh?" Lewis shook his head. "Too much seasalt in this batch. Send a memo to Uncle Frank."

Beneath his seat a memo-dispatching machine whirred briefly to life.

Despite the excess of natural seasoning, Lewis chomped up all the contents of the eight-ounce bag and asked for another. While he was working on that second one his private and non-buggable pixphone buzzed.

"Well?" Lewis said to his chair.

"Sorry, boss," said the chair, in a voice very similar to his, as it wheeled him over to the pixphone alcove.

"Who?" Lewis said toward the phone, wiping at his badly-shaved chin with his usable hand.

"Call from Barsetshire, England, boss," the pixphone informed him in its high-pitched voice.

"That dimwit quiff," said Lewis. "Okay, put her on. What the hell is wrong now, Onita?"

"I figured you ought to see this, Crackpot. It's—"

"I know what it is, you dimwit quiff. I had a copy two days ago."

The lean black girl on the phone screen was holding up a drawing of a mechanical device. "How come you're always jumping bad with me, Crackpot? I'm one of your better—"

"Stow it. Is that all you wanted?"

"I sure as scrap didn't want to ask after your health," Onita replied. "We got this diagram of the new anti-Gadget gimmick NRA-Great Britain is going to introduce. Did a lot of very high-class spy work to get it, matter of fact."

Crackpot made a diminishing gesture with his hand. "Okay, Nita, I know you people are well-intended."

"How'd you see the diagram already?"

"I just did," Crackpot told her. "I'm sending you guys a new schematic for building a new Gadget. It'll compensate for that new gimmick NRA's going to try. We stop it in England, and they're not going to bother to introduce it over here. Schematic'll come to you in the usual way."

"Okay, Crackpot," said the black girl. "You didn't shave so good today."

"Shaved myself this morning," he said. "That new parasite-shaver of mine has been getting too surly."

"You didn't have to build it so it could talk. Seems to me you like to have a certain—"

"Go snuff yourself, Nita. Get off my box. Bye."

"I wasn't trying to—"

He jabbed at the phone, killing the image. "Dimwit quiff," he murmured. "Well-meaning, though. Sort of pretty, too. I wonder if she and . . ." He didn't finish the sentence, instead leaning back in the chair and closing his puffy eyes. "Okay, okay. Get me Conway, if it's safe."

"At once, boss," said the pixphone. "Yep, it's safe. He's home, not monitored in anyway."

Crackpot still had his eyes closed when Conway's voice came out of the phone speaker. "Conway here."

"You've never been to England, jerk."

"Why, no, old chap, can't say I have. Eh?"

"Then why do you persist in talking like some dimwit Limey?"

"Jolly good point, Crackpot. I imagine it fits in with my image of myself, don't you know."

Crackpot opened his eyes, gave a small shudder. "You're an ugly man, Conway."

"Fancy I am, old thing," Conway admitted. He was very thin, round-shouldered. He had an enormous nose and huge ears. "Which may be why I do voiceovers down at the bally

Republic of Southern California News Network, do you see. And why I need the extra income your blinking clandestine salary brings me. Eh?"

"Rafe Santana is in Mexico, isn't he?"

"Righto, old bean."

The fat young man frowned. "What did they do to him in that medical dump?"

"Merely the usual pre-trip routine, old boy."

"Don't scrap me, Conway. I told you to find out what else they did to Santana."

"Nothing, not a bloody thing so far as I—"

"Why I use you is beyond me, you couldn't find your backside with a roadmap. I *know* something—"

"I tell you, Crackpot, that visit of Santana's was purely routine. For the blinking life of me I don't know why you're even interested in the bloke. How'd you find out about him anyway?"

"I just did," answered Crackpot. "Make one more try, Conway, being subtle if possible."

"I'll give it the old school try, Crackpot me lad, though if you could see your way clear to provide me with a bit more info to work—"

"Enough of you." He shut off his RSCNN contact.

The wheelchair took him away to the center of the underground room.

Crackpot again closed his eyes. He massaged his chin, frowning, trying to relax in the chair. "Come on, come on," he urged himself after a moment. "Let me see more than last time."

CHAPTER TEN

Susan Cereza moved all the way across the wide front seat of the bumping landvan. Arms folded beneath her breasts, long bare legs tucked under her, she watched the dry hilly country they were passing through.

"You don't like me because of my handicap," said the wiry young driver. "That's it, isn't it, chiquita?"

"Which handicap, Perdido?"

Perdido gave a bitter laugh, wanged his metallic right hand against the control panel. "This handicap," he said, "this *mano de estaño*. You don't realize how bitter life can—"

"I thought it was made of aluminum, not tin."

"You also do not understand I am a poet inside," complained Perdido.

"Inside perhaps."

"Not having two good hands, it's a real burden. A woman does not like to be fondled by metal fingers. And did you ever try to pick your nose with an aluminum finger, or clean out your ear?" Perdido shook his head sadly, thrusting his metal hand out the window.

Bam! Zizz!

A beam of sizzling light shot out of the tip of his forefinger, sliced the head off a large orange lizard who'd been sunning on a rock.

"That's six today, and not one miss," chuckled Perdido.

"You couldn't do that so easily with a flesh-and-blood hand, kill harmless creatures."

"True, chiquita," admitted Perdido. "I made up my mind, once the tragedy of being deprived of my hand had been visited on me, that my new *mano* would be an improvement on the old one. Which is why I have a blaster pistol built in, as well as several other highly useful attachments."

Susan, arms still folded, said nothing.

Perdido drummed on the control panel with his aluminum fingers. "I'll put my *mano* to use tonight."

"No, you won't. Gomes doesn't—"

"Gomes. He's only one of Carregador's flunkies. That for him."

Ping!

Perdido had snapped his metal fingers.

"There's to be no killing on this raid, Perdido, unless it's absolutely—"

"Necessary." He laughed. "It usually is, chiquita."

"The important thing is to get supplies from this Republic Army food depot. Not to—"

"I know my business," Perdido told her. "True it is I am not friends with gringo newsmen, but—"

"Rafe isn't exactly—"

"Oh, yes, that's right. He claims to be Mexican. And I forgot also he is the one true love of your life."

The dark-haired girl said, "Once."

"Still, I think. When you returned from your little rendezvous yesterday, chiquita, there were stars sparkling in your eyes, a look of—"

"Rafe Santana is going to help us. That's the only reason I contacted him."

"Oh, yes? I suppose that's why you wrote all those tearful letters to him before he came down here."

"The letters were requests for him to help us, nothing more."

"I had the impression they were filled with tender—"

"How do you know what was in my letters to Rafe?" She turned to stare at him.

Perdido shrugged. "My imagination, the imagination of a true poet, has told me."

"Once again your imagination has led you astray." Susan returned to watching the dusty road.

"So you don't care for Rafael Santana at all anymore?"

"No, not anymore."

"Then whatever happens to him, you won't be concerned."

"What do you mean, Perdido? What's going to happen to Rafe?"

"Oh, one can never tell what sort of evil may—"

Blam! Zizz!

"Ha, that makes seven."

"Rafe's on our side, as much as he can be, and he's not to be harmed."

"Yes, of course, chiquita," laughed Perdido. "You must forgive my vivid imagination, the curse of a one-armed poet."

Food-Lt. Waveny said, "Hey, I don't think this is so very funny."

"Sure, it's funny," Mr. Giggle assured him. "Do it again, Knuckles."

The silver-plated little android took up the cream-gun,

squirted ribbons of syncream into another pocket of Food-Lt. Waveny's tan trousers. "How's that grab your old wazoo?"

"I don't know really," said Waveny. "I mean, I'm willing to grant there are different sorts of humor in the world, still—"

"What do you think, soldier?" Mr. Giggle pointed a pink finger at Gourmet-1st Class Hootman.

Hootman, a long thin young man, was the only person sitting out in the audience section of the small rec hall of the food depot. "Well, I think humor has to be more topical."

Knuckles gave Food-Lt. Waveny another squirt, this one in the boot. "Look, puckeybrain, we've done our shows at two hundred and eight hospitals and sixty-five military bases around—"

"Don't you have," asked Gourmet-1st Class Hootman as he walked toward the small stage, "any girls in your act?"

"Don't you read *Variety?*" demanded Mr. Giggle. "Don't you know we're the hottest—"

"To me for really good topical comedy you must have girls with big mambos."

"Mambos?" inquired Knuckles, absently squishing syncream into his own ear. "What's a mambo?"

"You know, whamos, kaboopies, chugamuggas," amplified Hootman, making jiggling motions with both hands in front of his narrow chest.

"He must mean," realized Mr. Giggle, "mammywammies, chubbles, kazooms."

"What kind of nerfing act do you think we're doing. We're beloved by millions of frapping little kids. Do those little loyal-hearted tykes want to see kazooms?"

"I've been interested in that sort of thing since I was five or six," said Hootman.

"So have I," said Food-Lt. Waveny, "now you mention it. I recall when I was a lad in rompers I was fascinated with the really enormous boopies of my governess, a sensual wench who—"

"Stuff all this biographical crapola," shouted Knuckles, doing an impatient dance on the boards of the stage. "We're supposed to put on this frabbing show here tonight and all you two bozos are doing is throwing me curves. Now, we open with the Giggle and Knuckles medley, then we invite Waveny up on the stage, do the cream in the jeans business with his cake decorating gizmo and then we give the fighting men our—"

"Nobody here's actually a fighting man," corrected Food-Lt. Waveny. "Our whole fifty-six-man staff is made up of chefs, nutritionists, supply people. We do have some guards to defend the warehouse, but—"

"Fifty-six?" Mr. Giggle slapped his pink cheeks with his yellow-gloved hands. "You mean there are only fifty-six men in this whole setup?"

"We've been trying to get more."

"Cheez," said the little metallic Knuckles. "We come to this out-of-the-way puckeyhole to do our show and you only got fifty-six—"

"You're hardly the ones to criticize," Hootman said. "You ought to know what our boys in uniform like, a little touch of mambos to boost their morale."

"What a business," said Mr. Giggle. "Yesterday we get bawled out by the scrapping nuns just because Knuckles gooses the Mother Superior, now we get screamed at because we don't have any filthy stuff in our—"

"Nothing filthy about boopies," Food-Lt. Waveny said. "I, too, would rather watch some stunning young women with ample whammies than have my pockets filled with cake topping."

"You provincial puckeywits," Knuckles exclaimed, stamping his metal feet. "What do you know about what's funny? What do you know about satire?"

"Well, I know a pocket full of—"

Bam! Blam! Wam! Zizz!

"What the heck is that?" cried Mr. Giggle.

Waveny jumped from the stage and ran to the window. The twilight outside was filled with red and yellow flashes. "It's a raid," he said, "a guerrilla raid."

Knuckles sat down on the edge of the stage. "There goes our audience," he said.

CHAPTER
ELEVEN

Men were dying on all six screens.

"I can use some of #2," Edgar Allan Boskow was growling into a hand mike. "Give me a few seconds of #3."

Rafe stood back from the half dozen monitor screens. The real sounds of the skirmish outside did not reach them here inside their mobile-bunker.

Boskow, scratching at his frizzly beard, scanned the screens. "What the puckey is wrong with 'bot-camera #6. Is he chickenwitted? We're not getting anything screenable."

The view on Screen #6 showed the entire midday hillside where the fighting was taking place, the Republic of Southern California troops working their way up, the Mexican Army soldiers defending Position #26 atop the wooded hill.

"Get your tin butt in closer, #6," Boskow boomed into the mike.

Rafe, noticing a young Republic soldier suddenly turn black and fall on Screen #3, came closer to the view-wall. "Is this as close as we ever get?"

"Usually," answered the shaggy correspondent. "Once in awhile, if I'm planning one of my heart-tug spots, I venture onto the field to talk to some dying kid. Trouble is, with these new blaster rifles the Mexies are using our kids get fried too quick. Give me ten seconds of what you got, #4. Will you move in tighter, #6, damn it!"

"So we just stay in here and pick out our footage?"

"A lot better than getting fried." Boskow's head bobbed, taking in the combat action all six of the robot cameras were bringing in. "Ask Bruce Dingdarling to show you his backside some time. He decided to crawl along on a surprise attack on Position #13 when they—"

"Suppose I take a hand camera, see what I can do?"

"No, or Less will broil my *huevos*. I have to see to it you survive, Rafael."

Rafe took a few steps toward the padded bunker door. "I don't feel much more involved in the war than I did when I was holding down the damn Lightside Desk."

"You've got to use your imagination," advised Boskow. "Imagine what it's like out there, the crackle of the guns, the harsh smell of fried flesh, the . . . Hey, good! Give me what you're getting on #5. Listen, #6, I don't want any more establishing shots. Roll in tighter." He tugged his beard a few times. "You better start selecting your footage for your cast tonight. Otherwise you're going to have to take my leftovers."

Buzz! Brr!

A seventh screen came to life. This one on the opposite wall. The weary face of Clifford Less appeared. "Santana, are you there?"

Moving to a position where the pixphone could pick him up, Rafe answered, "Yeah, here I am at the front."

"You're not that naïve are you? Willing to get snuffed for a story. Trust me, Santana, you're plenty close enough to all that foolishness," said Less. "What I want you to do is come back here to Guaymas."

"I was planning to, right after I do my cast from our field studio tonight."

"Come back right now."

"Why? What's happening?"

"Vice-President Spurrier is down from the Republic," said his boss. "He wishes to be interviewed for your War Desk show tonight."

"He's not war news. Why do—"

"If I were in the prime of my youth and believed a newsman should risk his life on a story, I'd agree with you. However . . . we *have* to interview Spurrier. You do, Santana."

"Anybody can do it. You can do it."

"Not me, my dour face is never to appear on the screen, remember? Besides which, our esteemed Vice-Prez has requested you. I believe he's hoping to woo the MexAm vote in the next election."

Rafe inhaled slowly, exhaled slowly. "Okay, I'll catch the next filmship out of here."

"You're to meet him at the Yankee-Plaza Hotel at four," Less told him. "We'll have a 'bot-camera waiting for you in the lobby."

Nodding, Rafe backed away from the phone.

They were having the daily *piñata* smashing in the enormous cocktail lounge of the Yankee-Plaza as Rafe entered the lobby. The pseudoclay pig was smashed by a blindfolded Major General and some painted chunks and a few of the plyowrapped gifts came flying out into the chill lobby.

Rafe located his robot-camera standing beside a tall potted cactus and trying to ignore the assistant press agent of one of the commando units.

"It would make a socko story," the little freckled man was insisting. "It would make for a bamo piece of footage. Envision this . . . you dolly in on two powerful manly hands which are tightening around the throat of—"

"Let's go," Rafe told his camera.

"Oh, afternoon, Santana. I have a boomo idea for a little War Desk feature. So when I learned this camera was waiting for you I—"

"No, Ferguson." Rafe took one of the robot's arms.

"It would be bango, Santana. Envision this, if you will . . . We roll in on the sinewy, battle-scarred hands of a tough fighting commando as—"

"No, Ferguson. Now get out of our way or you'll go bango on your ass."

"No reason to get nasty, Santana. We're all members of the same prof—"

Rafe gave him a push which carried Ferguson over and caused him to sit in the cactus pot.

"You lousy spick, I don't have to take that."

Rafe let go the camera, whirled and stalked toward the little man.

"Ahum," cautioned the camera, rolling after him.

Rafe got control of himself, left Ferguson in the pot and escorted his camera over to the elevators.

By the time they stepped out on the eighteenth floor Rafe was breathing evenly again. "Fine guy they pick to represent the Republic down here, calls us . . . what the hell, no use."

Vice-President Spurrier was supposed to be staying in Suite 1803. Rafe and his man-high robot-camera stopped before the sky-blue door and he knocked.

Nearly a minute went by before the door swung open inward. "Come in," a soft voice invited.

Rafe let the camera go in ahead of him. The door closed and he saw Susan Cereza standing beside him. He raised his eyebrows, then smiled at her.

She didn't return the smile. "We're ready to go," she said.

CHAPTER
TWELVE

At the top of the ramp a rectangle of late-afternoon sunlight glowed.

"You shouldn't," said the handsome young man walking beside the wheelchair.

"Snuff yourself, Roger," said Crackpot.

"Down underground you're safe, Lewis. Go wandering around the countryside and you're liable to—"

"I can take care of myself. I've always been able to do that. In fact, I don't need you trailing after me right now."

"What I'm talking about is NRA," said his handsome cousin. "They'd love to catch you."

"They have no idea who I am, never will."

The chair rolled out into the huge white-gravel parking area. A landvan was parked a few yards from the ramp exit.

"There's no reason you have to go off to Mexico yourself." Roger opened the cab door of the van.

"There are reasons. I have to help someone."

"This Santana guy? You've never even met him, when you used to watch him on that 'Lightside' thing you made rude noises and—"

"Go away, leave me alone. I have to get going."

Roger bent to lift his cousin out of the wheelchair. "If you have to travel, I ought to go with you."

"Let the chair do it, clumsy."

"Sorry, Lewis."

"Good thing you're family, Rog. Otherwise I don't know where you could get hired." Crackpot used his good hand to depress several buttons on the side of his wheelchair.

The chair seat rose up until Crackpot was at the same level as the cab seat. He reached out, caught hold of the steering bar and tugged himself into the van.

Handsome Roger moved, hesitantly, to push the abandoned wheelchair out of the way. The chair anticipated him and moved itself.

Crackpot, grunting and puffing, was getting himself adjusted into the special driver seat.

"How do you know Santana's in trouble anyway?" Roger asked.

"I just know."

"What kind of trouble? You still haven't told me."

"Trouble I can help him out of."

"Why him? What's so special about some MexAm media guy?"

"Part of something bigger," Crackpot told him, "something I'm going to stop."

Roger came closer to the van. "Having a feud with National Robot & Android, playing pranks, is one thing, Lewis. Are you going to—"

"I haven't needed a nanny or a guardian since I was eleven, Rog. Go away and annoy somebody in the plants. I understand you and that chubby girl in the advertising wing are—"

His cousin laughed. "Okay, Lewis," he said. "How long will you be gone?"

"No way of telling."

"You really should take someone along."

"I run the entire Arundel Soyfood business and all its sub-sidiaries, Rog, and I also play, as you call them, pranks," said Crackpot as he shut himself in the cab. "By now you should be convinced I'm self-sufficient."

Roger stepped back, gave his cousin a mock salute.

Crackpot told the landvan, "Get me away from here."

Republic Army robots were loading food cartons onto hovering Mexx guerrilla skyvans, blaster rifles were buzzing, men were shouting. A small silver-plated android was help-ing out with the loading, weaving through the flashing dusk with a large sack of soyflour balanced on his head.

". . . RSC Army spokesmen made it clear that this daring twilight raid last night would not have been possible had not the guerrillas made use of the illegal devices known as Gadgets."

The face of Major General Mays replaced the raid footage on the dash newscreen. "This war will end sooner, our men will be home quicker, if we can stamp out the use of these infernal machines. If you know of anyone using, selling or manufacturing a Gadget, please turn that person or persons in to the authorities."

Crackpot, munching at a neochoc soycake, laughed.

The raid returned to the screen. "The Gadgets used by the vicious Mexican guerrillas were powerful enough to control all the Army warehouse 'bots as well as famed TV personality, Knuckles, beloved co-star of the 'Mr. Giggle & Knuckles' show. This dramatic footage, in fact, was filmed for us by the publicity robot-camera traveling with the brave little andy on his tour of hospitals and bases in war-torn Annexed Mexico."

"That little twit." Crackpot looked away from the screen and out at the bright Southern California afternoon. His landvan was taking him across ag country, through numerous acres of domed orchards.

"We sure hope all our boy and girl fans, as well as moms and dads, will be able to see Knuckles back on TV just as soon as possible." Mr. Giggle, tears tracing down his pink cheeks, was on the screen now. "That Gadget they used on him really upset the plucky little guy. He kept muttering subversive phrases and trying to tote boxes most of the night. All of you who'd like to send him get-well cards can address them to Art's Android Repair Shop, Guaymas, Annexed Mexico."

"Elsewhere in the war—"

"Off," Crackpot told the screen.

It went blank.

Crackpot, as best he could, relaxed in the driver seat. "Infernal machines, huh?" He laughed once more.

CHAPTER
THIRTEEN

They were all machines. The fishermen gathered around the log fire on the beach below, the guitar player sitting down in the flagstone courtyard, the smiling waiter who was crossing the twilit balcony. All of them androids.

Bowing, saying, "Here you are, señorita," the android waiter placed the cup of syncaf on the round tile table.

Her slender fingers resting beside the Gadget, Susan said, "Thank you, that'll be all. Unless . . ." She glanced over at Rafe.

"No, nothing," he said.

"I am at your beck and call from dusk until dawn," the smiling android assured her before leaving the wide balcony to return inside the villa.

Rafe was leaning against the balcony railing. "Hardly any other people here," he said.

"Exactly," the girl said. "The Posada Sombra was very exclusive even before the war began. Now very few people come here, most of them high-up Republic Army."

"We don't want to run into any of them."

"This is an off time. No military here, Rafe, and only a few other guests," explained Susan. "The staff is entirely andy, which is why all you need to control them is one of these Gadgets. You'll be safe waiting here."

"Waiting?"

"I have to leave you here a day or so. When we're absolutely certain everything is safe, you'll be picked up and taken to the meeting."

"Don't trust me?"

"I trust you, not everyone in Mexx feels the way I do. Besides which, you're not the only one we have to worry about." She picked up the coffee cup, cradled it in both hands. "That guitarist has played *Mia Cara* three times in a row." She touched the Gadget, pushed a knob.

The music ceased.

A warm wind was blowing across the black glazed water of the gulf, rattling the high palms which surrounded the courtyard of this villa and the dozen others which made up this section of the Posada Sombra complex. Lights showed in only one other villa.

"When you leaving?" Rafe asked.

"Soon." The night wind touched at her long dark hair.

"After you left the Republic," he said, "I was going to write to you."

"But?"

Hands in pockets, he faced her. "Seemed like putting flowers on a grave. It was over, so forget it and get on."

Susan sipped at the syncaf. "Yes, I felt more or less like that."

"I didn't, though, exactly forget."

The cup clicked as she set it on the mosaic tiles of the table top. "Rafe, do you think someone else got the letters I sent you?"

"The RSC Postal Authority misplaces a letter once in awhile. Maybe two or three." He was watching her, frowned at the frown he saw on her face. "Wait now, do you have something specific in mind? Do you know they were side-tracked?"

Susan said, "I don't know anything for certain about them. Writing you was probably a foolish thing to do, but I used a cover address on the envelope and, far as we know, your government hasn't been interrupting personal mail from Mexico. And yet . . ."

He took the other chair at the table. "You find out something lately?"

"One of the men, a boy almost, was hinting yesterday about what I'd said to you in those letters. He was kidding me about still being fond . . . probably nothing."

"They were supposed to be very businesslike, those letters."

Very carefully Susan reached across to put her hand over his. "Not completely," she said, her voice so low it was almost lost in the gentle wind. "I've been very much caught up in what we're trying to do . . . but sometimes . . . sometimes I missed you. Even after so many years."

"Too bad they didn't get through."

"Suppose the letters were intercepted?"

"I don't think they were. And what if somebody in the Republic intelligence setup did find out you and I know each other? Not exactly a secret, anyone who was at college with us would be aware of that."

"First I sent you the letters," she persisted, "then you were assigned to cover the war here in Mexico."

"A job I've been after a long time, Susan."

"Maybe I'm trying too hard not to be naïve. Maybe I'm too suspicious."

"Nobody followed me here," Rafe told her. "We're sure of that. No bugs or tracking devices were planted on my clothes or in my camera. You can be suspicious of me if you want, but I really am trying to help."

Her hand tightened on his. "I know, I know."

Rafe stood, moved around the table and lifted her to her feet. "What time do you have to be where you're going?"

"Not till morning actually."

He kissed her. The first time in a long time. Finally he said, "Let's go inside."

"Your robot-camera's in there."

"I'll send him out here," Rafe said.

He touched the doorknob and the door exploded. Exploded out at him, turning into thousands of needle-sharp splinters and every one jabbing into him, tearing at his skin, ripping it away.

A room full of people waited on the other side of the threshold. A hundred of them at least crowded around a long conference table, each dressed in the white clothes of field workers, faces brown and dusty. A heavyset man smiled, came toward Rafe, hand held out.

The man exploded when Rafe touched him. Bits of flesh, slivers of bone, splashes of blood hit Rafe, knocking him back. Back out of the room, out across the dry fields and under the dead trees.

Little silver men were dancing under the leafless trees. Dancing, laughing, turning handsprings. One of them fell, stayed sprawled on the cracked yellow earth.

Rafe bent to help him up. When he touched the gleaming little android it exploded. Great jagged shards of metal tore into Rafe's body, ripped chunks out of his flesh.

Someone was coming to help him. A slim girl, naked, long black hair whipping in the wind which was sweeping across the darkening field.

It was Susan, a white knobbed sphere glowing in her right

hand. She smiled a slow smile, then said something. She was a long way off, but coming closer swiftly.

She must not touch him.

Rafe realized that now. Anyone who touched him would die. He didn't mind about the others, but Susan must not die.

"Get away," he said and she didn't hear.

She kept smiling, coming to him.

"Get away! Get away! GET AWAY!"

He reached out to take hold of her. His hand touched twisted sheets.

In the early morning light of the villa bedroom Rafe, coming fully awake, saw the note on her pillow.

Though he hadn't seen her writing for seven years he recognized it, that and the faint sandalwood fragrance left behind.

"I had to leave. You'll be contacted," said the note. "I love you."

He smiled as he read the note. But then he remembered the dream.

CHAPTER FOURTEEN

"Golly, that sounds great," said Howie Peet, the youthful director of the United Federation Secret Police. "Who came up with a really nifty idea like that?"

"Don't bounce that way," Edgar Allan Boskow told him.

There were five men in the one-way neoglass dome, four of them frowning and scowling at Peet.

"Was I bouncing? Gee, I'm sorry. I'll try to sit up straight and not jiggle." Folding his hands in his lap, he smiled hopefully at the others. "Turning this Mexican fellow into a human bomb is a really great notion, though. We'd like to do something like that at SP. Would we be infringing on your patent if we borrow—"

"You don't patent a clandestine device like the implant-bomb, Peet," said Major General Mays.

"Oh, yeah, I get it. Then it wouldn't be a secret." He giggled, unfolded and refolded his hands. "SP ought to think of these great ideas first. I'm really glad I came out here from the East to sit in on this get-together."

Boskow had been gazing out at the early morning hills which ringed their secluded meeting room. "According to our source of Mexx information," he resumed, "Rafe Santana should be meeting with Carregador, Gomes and at least five other Mexx people within forty-eight hours. Right now he's waiting at Posada Sombra, our monitoring device in the implant tells us that."

Peet, scratching at his tweedy armpit, asked, "How come we know so much about Mexx? I came in late so—"

"Don't fidget," suggested Major General Mays.

"Golly, I always do that when I'm excited," said young Peet. "This implant-bomb of yours is really an exciting breakthrough. You're sure Santana has no idea he's got the thing ins—"

"If he knew," put in the black agent of the Republic of Southern California Security Bureau, "he wouldn't be going through with this job for his network. He'd be running to a hospital to get the frapping thing unplanted."

"Rafael Santana," said Major General Mays, "is not the first of our personnel missiles. In none of the prior instances was the carrier aware of the implant at all. The actual bomb-monitor unit is very tiny, the surgical work done on him was quite expert."

Peet clapped his hands, then gave an apologetic smile. "Terrific, just terrific."

The fifth man at the circular table was the District Chief of Covert Activities, a small man named Oscar Kipling. "Sometimes I have my doubts about the ethics involved in using an unsuspecting guy like—"

"We have to get rid of Carregador," said the major general. "You agreed on that."

"Yes, I have no objection to his being killed," said Kipling. "Still, if we have someone inside the Mexx camp we might as easily try another method of—"

"It was decided the personnel bomb was the best solution to the problem," reminded the major general.

"Boy, I can't see anything wrong with sacrificing a single guy if it means wiping out the whole damn Mexx guerrilla hierarchy," said Peet, commencing to bounce.

"Exactly—stop that idiot bouncing—how we feel," the major general said. "With Carregador and Gomes dead and gone we can concentrate on the Mexican forces without being harassed by guerrillas."

"I don't think murdering the leaders means stopping the guerrillas," said Kipling. "They'll find new leaders."

"Blowing up Carregador is only one part of our operation," Mays said.

Peet forgot himself and bounced. "Gosh, this is a terrific strategy. We could make use of something similar back East. Will you guys pass along the secret of your implant-bomb before I—"

"I'll plant one in your kazoo if you don't stop interrupting," warned Boskow. "You're supposed to be an observer, Peet, not an active participant."

"Well, gee, I don't see why you guys are so down on a little sincere enthusiasm. Let me remind one and all that someday, maybe soon, your Republic'll be governed by the United Federation. Then you won't be able to pick on me so much. Not that I mind a little good-natured kidding."

"Shut up," suggested Major General Mays.

"Using someone well known in the media," said Kipling, "may not be too wise."

"Our network contacts went along with the utilization of Santana," said Mays.

"Blowing up a newsman sets a bad precedent," Kipling said.

"No one," said Boskow, "will ever know we had anything to do with the incident." He twisted his fingers in his beard.

"Santana, let's not forget, is one of the few outsiders who's got a chance to get close to Carregador. Look, Kip, I don't feel so very jolly about this. Rafael's a buddy of mine, you know. A nice guy. A little too pro-Mexican, but that's to be expected sometimes in a Mexican. The point is, once Susan Cereza started writing those letters to him it was obvious here was somebody who could be used."

"Hey, do you guys waylay mail, too?" Peet was bouncing, clapping his hands together. "I'm really glad to hear that. I've been trying a little mail tampering back East, and you ought to hear the complaining I get from some of those—"

"As soon," said the major general, "as we know Santana is at the meeting and all the Mexx leaders are there, the implant-bomb will be activated."

"Won't be more than two days from now," said Boskow. "Then we'll be a lot closer to ending this unfortunate war."

"Don't you really like the war?" asked Peet. "Seems to me, gosh, it's pretty exciting, what with the . . ."

Arnold Bennish blundered through the steam. "Excuse me," he said, realizing he'd walked into a group of seated men.

"No harm done, bub," said the scraggly old man who materialized in front of him. "Park your toke and have a swig." A plyobottle of thick yellowish wine was thrust toward him.

"You're not supposed to have your clothes on in here." The Head Troubleshooter for NRA had noticed the old man and his three grubby companions were fully dressed, as fully dressed as their tattered garments allowed. "In fact, your class of people shouldn't be in the Beverly Hills Sector Health Complex Spa at all."

"Don't worry," said another of the tattered old men, "we won't get caught or nothing."

"Allow me to introduce our congenial little crowd," said the old man with the yellow wine. "I am Futuristic Slim and, reading from left to right, you have Salinas Sector Shorty, Bodega Red and Professor Stun."

Bennish, who was dressed only in a fuzzy pseudocloth towel, said, "There aren't supposed to be any bums in here. That's a—"

"Nix, nix," advised Bodega Red, "don't futz. Keep subdued."

"The fewer andies we got to control, the better," explained Futuristic Slim.

"A Gadget!" Bennish suddenly realized. "You seedy bastards are using a Gadget! What kind of incredible nerve do you possess to come in here and use a Gadget in front of National Robot & Android's top trouble—"

"Tip him the rod, Prof," said Futuristic Slim.

Professor Stun, a very thin and very tall old man, reached over to touch Bennish with his left hand. The hand consisted of a dented coppery stunrod.

Bennish dropped down on the steam-room floor, went sliding across the tiles.

Some time later, over an hour it turned out, someone knelt beside the sprawled Bennish. "Would you be Mr. Bennish?" inquired Roger Arundel, Crackpot's handsome cousin. "Sorry I'm late, but we had some trouble in the soypopping department."

"Oy," groaned Bennish. "You derelicts better . . . oy, what kind of stunrod did those bastards use?"

"Afraid I can't tell you, Mr. Bennish. You are Mr. Bennish, aren't you? We had an appointment to meet at this—"

"Yeah, yeah." With Roger's help the troubleshooter sat up. The steam seemed even thicker than before. "Got away, the whole tacky crew. We've got to stop the Gadget or the scum of the earth will be intruding in every country club and health spa in the country."

Roger grinned. "I can be of some aid there, Mr. Bennish."

"You're Roger Arundel, huh?"

"I am." Roger got him over to a tile bench.

"You told my field man you know who Crackpot is. He thinks you really do."

"Yes, I do." Roger's grin broadened. "I know who he is, I know where he is. I can tell you how to catch him."

"NRA can pay you, if you're not simply another con artist, $25,000 for that information."

The handsome Roger sat down next to the troubleshooter. "My price is ten times that. $250,000."

"That's completely ridiculous. NRA isn't going to give you anything like—"

"Then NRA can go on losing $6,000,000 a year."

Bennish grunted. "Okay, when we get Crackpot you get $250,000."

"I want $50,000 right now or we don't have anything more to talk about."

After another sad grunt Bennish stood up. "Let's go find my clothes," he said.

CHAPTER FIFTEEN

Nelson Hackensacker, Jr., said, "Yack," and pushed aside his mug of neococoa.

"A thousand pardons, effendi, if I have offended you in some—"

Bong!

The white-enameled robot had bowed low to express his chagrin and clunked his top section into the kidney-shape desk.

"That cocoa tastes like mundungus," complained the old man.

"I am covered with a million forms of mortification, sahib," the attendant robot assured him. "I'll taste the offending brew myself to determine exactly why—"

"You can't taste it, dunderhead. You don't have a mouth or tastebuds."

Bong! Clong!

"And cease bowing and scraping. What is it, Burton?"

The dark chubby man was in the entry way of the Chairman of the Board of National Robot & Android's private office. "It's about this month's bribes," he said, taking a few cautious steps into the oval room.

"Turn the checks over to the check-signing 'bot, you kirkbuzzer."

"The thing is, a good many of our bribe requests have gone up sharply." He held out his chart-projector. "I brought along some graphs which—"

"Just tell me, I don't want to see any more of your quockerwodger charts and graphs."

"Well, for instance, Spain2 wants $100,000 instead of the usual $75,000," said Burton. "It seems the Gadget has been spreading rapidly through Spain2 the past few weeks. The profits from their cut of all our NRA mechanisms are dropping."

Slurp! Splash!

"I told you not to try drinking that bilge, now you've got it all over your front."

Bong!

"I prostrate myself on the altar of your anger, effendi. I—"

"Go someplace else."

"Of course, sahib. You have but to breathe a wish and I—"

"Both of you."

The two enameled attendant robots slunk for the side door.

"Oughtn't you to," asked Burton, "have at least one medical attendant around at all time? Just in case."

"In case of what?" asked old Hackensacker.

"Well . . ."

"I suppose all the chowderheads we bribe to use our machines exclusively now want bigger helpings?"

"All except Portugal."

"They're too stupid to be venal. Turn on one of the wall sets."

"Shouldn't we discuss these bribes first?"

"President Sturdy of the United Federation is due to make a policy speech," said Hackensacker. "They tell me he may say something about NRA and our Gadget problem."

Burton, chart-projector held under an elbow, clicked on the largest of the ten viewing screens on the pale blue wall. "It's possible we'll get federal funding in our fight against the Gadget."

"Yes, and openly this time."

". . . here he is, ladies and gentlemen, the first openly gay president in the history of our great land. Don Sturdy."

"What's that prettywilly up to now?" demanded Hackensacker when Sturdy's image took over the screen.

The United Federation president was leaning against the presidential throne wearing an aluminum-cloth party gown and a blond wig. "I'm throwing away my prepared text," he announced, flinging a sheaf of pink pages over his bare shoulder, "in order to talk to you, my fellow citizens, about the terribly exciting grand ball we're going to be having here at the Presidential Palace next week. I'm letting you have a little sneak look at my—"

"Off!" shouted the old man. "Get that fruitcake off my set."

"He might get around to NRA."

"Off!"

When the screen was dead again Burton said, "Shall we return to the bribe situation?"

Buzz! Buzz!

"What?" The old man said toward his desktop pixphone.

The head and shoulders of Arnold Bennish appeared. "Good news," he said.

"We're not upping your budget again, so you can quit fawning."

"There's no need," said the troubleshooter. "Though you'll probably be wanting to hand me a fat bonus."

"A bonus? For what?"

"For catching Crackpot and putting him out of business." The old man began ticking in his chair. "You have him?"

"I'll have him before the day is over."

"You're absolutely certain?"

"Yeah, absolutely," said Bennish. "Crackpot is a very strange young guy named Lewis Arundel, a cripple since he was a kid. Family's very big in soy out here. Apparently he's got some kind of grudge against NRA and, being an electronics genius, he came up with the Gadget as a way of doing us harm."

"I might want to talk to the young man," mused old Hackensacker.

"I'll have him back there by tomorrow morning. He's on his way to Mexico, driving alone in a landvan," said the NRA troubleshooter. "I've set up a plan for waylaying him."

Hackensacker asked, "How'd you get on to him?"

"His cousin sold him out."

The old man nodded. "Good, you can always count on family betrayals paying off. Good."

Meanwhile all across the Western Hemisphere the furtive use of the illicit Gadgets continued.

In the Palm Springs Sector of Greater Los Angeles, for instance, a naked seventeen-year-old girl was skulking through a twisting, dipping tinted plyo halltube, one hand kneading the small of her smooth tan back. She was a pretty girl with long turquoise-colored hair. She was tattooed in several places, chiefly with small detailed depictions of Western scenes—Indians attacking the cavalry, covered wagons rolling Westward, gunfighters shooting it out at the height of the day. Each vignette had the slogan *Property of Rance Keane* incorporated in it.

"He don't like for you to go traipsing around unclothed,

ma'am," reminded one of the androids who stood along the tube. "Ceptin' for him, a'course."

"Blow it out your tailpipe," suggested the naked girl.

"My particular model android doesn't contain a . . . *bop!*" The android, who was a very reasonable replica of the real Rance Keane, suddenly stopped functioning.

The girl smiled, which somehow caused her small breasts to jiggle in an affirmative way, and continued on toward the main entryway to Rance Keane's #2 Villa. When she reached the solid neosteel door there were full seven of the Keane simulacra frozen in her wake.

"Tsk, tsk," said the door. "Naked as a jaybird, and twicet as cute. Dadgum if you ain't . . . *zunk!*"

The door stopped talking, swung open.

Bright sun and hot dry desert air flowed in.

The girl stared out at the almost empty countryside, hollering, "Olley olley oxen free!"

Nothing resulted.

"Come on, come on, time's a-wasting."

Then, from behind a lone joshua tree stepped a blond young cyborg in a sleeveless two-piece treksuit. "Not so loud," he mouthed as he came trotting over to her. "You oughtn't to holler so loudly, Trinity."

"You sound exactly like one of his androids," said Trinity Keane. "'Don't go flaunting around with your bummy hanging out, ma'am,' 'Zip up your front, ma'am,' and such like and so on."

"'Don't commit adultery, ma'am,'" added the young man, scanning the blank hot desert behind him. "Are those real vultures up there?"

"Robots," replied Rance Keane's greenheaded wife. "Now get on in here, Pete." She hooked a bare arm around his neck, yanked him into the tube with her.

"These clandestine *tweet* meetings are starting to play havoc with my *tweet* nerves, Trinity," Whistlin' Pete Goodwin told the unclothed girl.

"I wish it wouldn't make you whistle." She let go his neck, grabbed his hand and hurried him along the tinted halltube. "I don't know why I keep falling for show business men exclusive. Though one of our therapy boxes suggests it has something to do with my late mother being a freefall acrobat and my possible daddy a steamfitter at a mechanical piano factory. If indeed he's the stud who slipped the old—"

"Trinity, *tweet* I love to . . . well, um, you know, have . . . well, *tweet* physical congress with you . . . but *tweet*, Trinity, I don't . . . like all this smutty talk."

"No? The harpist I was balling before you doted on it." She scratched her bare stomach, just above the depiction of Custer's Last Stand, with the hand holding the Gadget. "One occasion he got so darn excited he tried to bring his harp to bed with—"

"There *tweet* you go again," complained Whistlin' Pete.

"Oh, Petey, if only you'd learn to accept people as they are." They reached the end of the tube. She pressed another knob on the white ball and the heavy neocopper door swung inward. "You don't catch me nagging about how you're all the time whistling. Even though you go tooting at the very moment of—"

"Whistling is my profession," he reminded as he followed her, somewhat on tiptoe, across the circular living room of her husband's villa. His head ducked instinctively as he passed each temporarily incapacitated Rance Keane android guard. "I'm an artist, so you should not—"

"You got to admit, Petey, it's unusual for a fellow to start whistling out of his elbow when he and his lady love are in the very act of—"

"Okay, some of my built-in whistling equipment isn't perfect," admitted the entertainer. "You have to expect that with sensitive mechanisms."

"And as if the darn elbow weren't bad enough, I also get serenaded by your armpit, your navel, your knee, your—"

"Don't blame me for getting excited when we're together."

Trinity halted on the threshold of one of the bed chambers. "Hey now, Petey, you've actually come right out and told me I excite you."

"Well, sure *tweet*. Why else do I risk death and dishonor, and suffer a very sticky hike across the sands of the desert from the nearest skyport, to be *tweet* with you? You are absolutely certain he's not going to *tweet* pop in on us this afternoon?"

"Naw, he's with his agents. Don't worry. They're ironing out the details for a tour of Mexico, to entertain the troops." She let go of Whistlin' Pete, went bounding into the circular bedroom. "As if those poor guys don't get enough shooting down there." Trinity, toes wiggling, poised on the rim of the bedpit. She leaped in. "I won't be going south of the border with him. So we can have a lot more time together soon, Petey."

"I've been *tweet* thinking." He slouched to the lip of the oval pit, watching the sleek girl bouncing, her tattooed pictures blurring, on the oval sleepmat five feet below. "Seems to me *tweet* I maybe owe it to my country to entertain our fighting men, too. Since I never fought myself I—"

"You can't fight. Nobody wants a soldier whose navel is like to go off at the wrong time," she said. "Forget all this patriotic stuff, Petey." She held the Gadget above her head, depressed a button.

"Trinity? What did you just do?" asked Whistlin' Pete, squatting and frowning. "I feel sort of odd."

"It won't affect your powers as a romantic person at all. All I did was fix it so you won't whistle for a while."

"Can you do that with one of those things?"

"Yep. Let's proceed, huh?" she urged. "Come on down."

After a nervous scan of the room, Whistlin' Pete jumped.

Simultaneously, in the Pasadena Sector of Greater Los

Angeles, a skyvan came skimming low over the slanting thatched roofs and spires of the Wee Forge in the Briars. It circled the vine-covered buildings, as one of the red brick chimneys puffed out a swirl of blackish smoke and glittering sparks into the afternoon. The large digital neon sign over the neooak doors changed numbers so it now read *Over 1,260,963 Processed!* The van hovered a few feet above the slanting lawn of the place, a door popped open and six very old men jumped out. A young man in a five-piece bizsuit unfurled a dismount ladder and climbed, holding tight, after them to the ground.

"Oh, no. Oh, my, no." A solid-black robot came rolling out of a side door of the Wee Forge in the Briars. "That's real grass, absolutely real grass you're trampling. We don't, can't possibly allow it. And, at the same time, allow me to temper my criticism with an expression of our sincerest sympathy in your hour of bereavement. Now off the—"

"They're my great uncle's former service buddies," the young man told the funeral robot. "He was in the paratroopers, back in some war in the twentieth century. They all jumped out of the skyvan like that as a sort of gesture."

"A gesture?"

"Well, maybe if you weren't a paratrooper yourself it—"

"Look at this particular little old gentleman." The black-enameled robot was pointing a dark finger at one of the half dozen. "He's got some sort of hobnails on the bottoms of his wretched boots."

"We're all going to miss old Dan," said the bent, leathery old man with the offending boots.

"It wasn't Dan who kicked off," said another of the ancient paratroopers. "Collect your wits, Bert."

"Will you all follow me, please, into this side entrance," requested the funeral robot. "Tred very gently, extremely gently."

"Who's dead? It ain't Dan."

"It was Sam."

"Sam? Hell, I wouldn't of jumped out of that thing to honor Sam. Sam was my *bête noire* at the Veterans' Enclave Hospital. I wouldn't jump off a tipped-over urinal for Sam. Sam was—"

"Come along, come along." The robot, taking very cautious steps, was making his way up the lawn. "This is *real* grass, absolutely authentic."

"Who'd he say was deceased?" asked another of the senior paratroopers.

"Sam," said the young man. "It's my great uncle, Sam Dillingham. You six guys are supposed to be pallbearers."

"What?" The one with the hobnail boots stopped, stomped his foot on the authentic grass. "You mean to tell me that for Sam, of all people, I got to risk life and limb by jumping out of a skyvan and then on top of that I got to take a chance at a hernia dragging his darn coffin around?"

"It's a little box. Only a little plastic box with his ashes in it."

In the shadowy, sweet-smelling hallway an android was waiting. He had a pink face, blond curly hair and wore a long white robe. "Gentlemen, allow me to convey my deepest sympathies. I am a Model 207XR Nondenominational Reverend. I'll be officiating at the brief but touching ceremony . . . um . . . I find myself with a slight problem." He motioned the nephew aside, led him into an alcove where a fountain was spewing multicolored water. "You're the relative of the deceased?"

"Yes. What—"

"I've officiated at over two thousand cremations since I was installed here at the Wee Forge in the Briars . . . uh . . . but, young fellow, this is the first time I've had to deliver a farewell sermon about anyone who died in a bordello. Frankly, I'm stumped. Perhaps if I tried a few—"

"Plenty of time for that later." The black-enameled robot, after showing the ancient paratroopers to another room, came over to tap the young man on the shoulder. "According to our records, you ordered the Low Budget $12,000 Funeral for your late uncle."

"It's sufficient I think, especially since—"

"The point is, sir, you haven't paid so much as a penny, not one cent. The credit number you provided turns out to be spurious, further—"

"Don't worry." From a coat pocket the young man produced a Gadget, much like the one he'd given his late uncle. "You're not going to make a frumus, are you? No, you're going to go tell your computer it's all been paid for. The whole thing, including a small wake afterward for those old guys."

"Why, yes. Certainly. Was there some doubt?" The somber-hued robot bowed, departed. "Curtain time is three minutes, by the by."

"As for the elegy," the young man told the mechanical priest as he pressed a new button on the white sphere, "go ahead and talk about the bordello. It'll cheer everybody up."

And just about then in Mexico, a few miles behind the lines, Gossip-1st Class Claxton came strolling into the squat adobe offices of the *Battle Flag*. He was humming, both hands behind him. "Got it," he said, "and it works."

Editorial-Lt. Thorkin lifted his head from his scrutiny of the row of newstypers. "Not another of those obscene holy statues? I don't think, after seeing St. Joseph, I care to—"

"No, this is something useful." Claxton, a bony, brownish man, skirted the square man-high censor box which stood near the editor's desk.

"Hum," said the sturdy censoring mechanism. "Typer 3's current story not acceptable. Too many civilian casualties in that story. Cut."

Claxton, lips slightly puckered, perched on the edge of the editorial desk of the army newspaper. He moved the package he had behind his back to his knee. "Bought this down in Flea Market #6, and the damn thing works like a—"

"Hum," said the censor out of its midsection voice box, "no profanity on the part of army newsmen is allowed. I might also suggest you sit on a chair rather than the desk top."

Claxton unwrapped his Gadget. "Bet you won't approve of this either." He squeezed a knob down.

"Hum, I . . . *pok!*" The big box quivered, went dead.

"Hey!" Thorkin jumped up. "We can't go around—"

"Sure, we can. Now I have a Gadget we can control this bastard. We can print what we want."

"We can get busted down to Crossword Puzzler-2nd Class."

"Naw." Claxton stroked the white knobby ball. "All we have to do is say, if there's any flap, the censor box was malfunctioning. We didn't realize it. So in all innocence we went right ahead, wrote and printed stories we now realize were not in the best taste."

"Best taste? You know damn well somebody up in GLA is going to charge we committed treason."

"Yeah, but we blame it on him." His booted foot swung out to kick the censor in the side. "He didn't complain, so we assumed what we were printing was okay. You know, stuck down here in a strange land for untold months, stunned by the continual roar of battle, we maybe lost our perspective."

Sitting down slowly, the *Battle Flag* editor said, "I could handle the story about that last Mexx food raid the way I want."

"We can talk about what's happening to the civilians in the fighting zones."

"I could try the Food Corps kickback story, the use of prohibited weapons stuff, the—"

"Anything." Claxton tossed the Gadget on his palm. "We can print anything."

Thorkin reached over and patted the Gadget. "Okay. We'll try it . . . for a while."

While in Guaymas, during this same period of time, Fulmer Anderson was slouching across the gangplank from his floating restaurant to the shore. He was clad in a one-piece buff afternoonsuit, one of his big hands thrust deep in a side pocket. "Fame, fame, fame," he was crooning to himself while he hurried up a cobbled street.

The nearer he came to his goal, the more people there were around him, all heading in the same direction.

"Fame, fame, fame," sang the restaurateur-author. "Keeps alluding me, keeps alluding me."

Zizz! Blam!

"There he goes!"

"Get him! Fry him!"

Blasters crackled, stunguns hummed.

A Mexican, darkly clad, ducked into an alley. Two men in yellow uniforms were chasing him.

"Who is it?"

"What's wrong?"

"Mexx guerrilla I think," said someone near Anderson.

"Sí, that's what one of the store guards shouted," somebody else said. "Fellow tried to use a Gadget, to steal supplies out of the AmericaMecca."

Anderson swallowed, slowed. A half block directly ahead loomed the vast AmericaMecca store he'd been aiming for. Above the eggshell-white halfdome huge throbbing light-signs announced *AmericaMecca Market! Bringing the USA to the World! Junk Food! Gimcrack! Shoddy Appliances! Marked-Up & Unsafe Drugs! Hundreds of Other Worthless & Dangerous Items!*

Anderson's grip on the Gadget in his pocket slackened.

Blam! Blam! Zizzle!

"They got him!"

"I saw it! Didn't you see him stiffen!"

"Let's get a look!"

Anderson swung out of the procession to the doorways of the AmericaMecca store. "Another try for a little more fame thwarted," he murmured, feet dragging over the stone paving of the narrow side street.

He'd tried it at smaller shops and stores. But without the big outlets such as AmericaMecca his plan wasn't going to do much good. Anderson had been, for about a month now, using his Gadget to induce order department robots and servos to stock his novels. He'd been anticipating being able to place a large order for the Masochist, Sadist and Mr. & Mrs. Lust series at AmericaMecca this afternoon. He was anxious to see his works everywhere, not, though, at the risk of getting shot or even chased by security people.

"Boy, fate sure," he said now as he forlornly returned to his floating restaurant, "puts a lot of stumbling blocks in the path of the artist."

CHAPTER SIXTEEN

"Strangely deserted," observed Crackpot as his landvan took him off the highway into the landlot of Fat Ed's Mexicali Fly 'N Drive Inn. "Been looking forward to trying this place, too."

There were only three landcars on the vast lot, not more than five skycars up on the immense pole-supported pad above the circular restaurant. The giant Fat Ed statue turned slowly on the red tile roof, shaded by the circular landing pad.

"Welcome to Mexico, *amigo*," said the mustached robot who came rolling toward the cab of Crackpot's van.

The plump young man was scowling. "Should be more people here at this hour," he said. "Maybe the food's no good anymore."

"You should see us in one more hour, when the sky-truckers hit." The robot had stopped outside his window. It wore a neostraw sombrero, a plyoserape.

Crackpot was surveying the late afternoon lot. "I have a feeling . . ."

"Best food in Mexico, *amigo*." The robot held a finger up and the scent of hot chile came wafting out. "How about a Fat Ed Big Deal?"

Hesitating a few seconds, Crackpot asked, "What's the Fat Ed Big Deal?"

The robot caught its serape by the fringe and lifted it. Printed on its metal chest in glowtype was the menu. "The Fat Ed Big Deal is explained hereon," it said. "Consists of a heaping bowl of Fat Ed's famous Texas-style chile with big juicy chunks of soymeat swimming in—"

"Why is it Texas style?"

"Ah, there you have put your finger on a sore spot, señor," confided the robot. "Were it up to me, being a loyal native born Mexican mechanism, I would put only Mexican-style chile on the bill of fare. However, most of the *turistas* favor Texas style because—"

"Okay, never mind. I can read the rest of what I want to know off your stomach."

At the top of the menu was printed: *Ask About Today's Special!*

"What's today's special?"

"Oh, *tengo verguenza*," said the robot. "We don't have a special today. This is the why and the wherefore of that. Early this morning as the friendly Mexican sun appeared over yonder hills the chef-computer—"

"Forget it, forget it. Bring me the Fat Ed Big Deal."

"I will be most . . ." The robot all at once looked upward. "Hit the deck!" It threw itself flat out on the lot, sombrero flying away.

Crackpot saw them, too. Five dark skycars dropping down from directly overhead. Giving himself a whap on the side of the head, he said, "Why didn't you let me have more of a warning? What kind of precognition is it that can't see a trap coming."

"Crackpot, we know who you are!" boomed an amplified voice from above.

"We're requesting you to come out of there with your hands up."

"Wait a minute, schmuck, this kid's supposed to be a cripple."

"Nobody told me. I mean, I'm used to giving the standard pitch. Come out, hands up. That's the way it usually goes."

Crackpot told his van, "Get me away from here."

Nothing happened. They sat where they were.

"Pull back the fake roof," he ordered, "and aim the blaster cannons."

Nothing happened.

"Using disablers on me," Crackpot said. "Expensive, must be National Robot & Android themselves."

"Do you hear us, Lewis Arundel?"

The five dark skycars were landing, forming a tight circle around him.

"We want you to come with us."

"Any resistance will be met with force."

Crackpot sat watching the skycars settle in outside. "They know my name, they know I was planning to stop here." Again he jogged his head. "You didn't warn me about Cousin Roger either. All these dimwit messages about Rafe Santana and you don't once tell me my own cousin is a Judas."

"We advise you to make some sign of surrender, Crackpot."

Shifting in his chair, Crackpot managed to grip his unusable hand with his good hand. He gribbed tightly, closing his eyes.

Arnold Bennish said, "Ha," and rubbed his palms together.

"How shall I phrase the rest of this, sir?" asked the tall, black man seated next to him in the cabin of the skycar. "I've never apprehended a handicapped criminal before."

Bennish grabbed the talkstick away from him. "What kind of private police are you guys? I assumed you had some experience when I hired you to augment my staff."

"We do have a lot of experience, sir. But it hasn't been with handicapped—"

"Listen to me, Crackpot," Bennish yelled into the talkstick, "I want you to open your door and start climbing out of that van."

"Can he do that?"

"He can do it, his cousin assured me."

"You know, there aren't that many handicapped criminals in the world, which is why we don't know exactly how—"

"We haven't disabled your cab door, Crackpot. Open it!"

The black private cop leaned closer to the tinted window of their skycar cabin. "Oh, good, there it goes."

The door of Crackpot's van had come popping open.

"Start climbing out," instructed Bennish. "There are stunguns aimed at you, so don't try anything unusual, you scum!"

"Do you find that helps at all? To call criminals scum? We've been experimenting lately with more polite forms of—"

"Let's get moving, Crackpot!"

"You know," said the black man, "I don't see him anymore. He's not in his seat."

Bennish dropped the talkstick. "Trying some kind of god damn trick." He dashed to the door. Out in the waning afternoon he ran for the silent van. Before he reached the open-hanging door there was a blaster pistol in his right hand. "I want you alive, Crackpot, but if you try anything too smart I'll do you in."

No response from the cab, no tricks.

Bennish, chewing at his lower lip, peered up into the van. There was no one in the cab.

The NRA troubleshooter scrambled up and in.

The driver seat was empty, the passenger seat was empty.

"Crackpot," said Bennish, "we've got you hemmed in. Wherever you're hiding, there's no way for you to get clear of this lot."

He tried the handle of the door leading back into the body of the van. It was frozen, disabled by the equipment in the skycar Bennish had left, the door wouldn't open.

The passenger side door was inoperative, too.

Bennish dropped out of the cab. He trotted around the van, gesturing at his men in the waiting and watching skycars. "Did any of you bastards see him come out?"

Several of the NRA troubleshooters and private cops joined him on the Fat Ed parking lot.

"Nobody left that van, chief."

"Yeah, that's right. Not anybody."

Bennish made a snorting sound. "Okay, then Crackpot is still inside this van someplace."

But he wasn't.

CHAPTER
SEVENTEEN

Oscar Kipling made another slow circuit of Less' office suite. "Ah, here's one more." He squatted to detach a tiny black monitoring device from the underside of the robot bar.

Less' weary face grew several degrees sadder. "You mean I've had six bugs in this place and didn't know it? The network unbugging squad swore I was clean as a—"

"These are fairly sophisticated bugs, Less." Kipling stomped on his latest find with his heel, grinding it into minute electronic scrap. "Your people wouldn't notice most of these and, since several of them are on the Republic payroll, they possibly overlooked a couple of the more obvious bugs deliberately."

Less hunched down farther in his chair. "How is it you can spot them?"

The District Chief of Covert Activities tapped the side of his head. "By using the old towkas. I had a very efficient bugfinder implanted in my skull shortly after I took over my current job. Had to have it improved and augmented twice so far."

Shivering, Less said, "I don't see how you can let anybody fiddle with your head."

"That's all the bugs." Kipling sat on a loveseat. "Now we can talk."

"You've got something you want leaked?"

"That's what I hope my colleagues will think, which is why I came to see you here instead of setting up a more secret and secluded meet," said Kipling. "I don't want what I tell you to hit the news at all. It's possible I shouldn't even tell you."

Less straightened up. "This is pretty convincing, Oscar," he said. "You've got me halfway convinced you're not simply going to give me the latest Republic baloney."

"This is about a man of yours, young fellow named Rafe Santana."

"You know where he is now, don't you? That is, where he's supposed to be going."

"I know where he's headed, and I know exactly where he is at this moment," said Kipling. "Rafe Santana is being utilized by the Republic of Southern California."

Less, after new wrinkles visited his face, nodded. "Yeah, that explains why Mexx had such an easy time spiriting him away," he said. "Faking that visit by our revered Vice-President Spurrier, getting in and out of the Yankee-Plaza so smoothly."

"We wanted Santana to reach the Mexx camp."

"You trying to tell me Rafe's a spy? I don't believe he—"

"He doesn't know anything about how he's being utilized. He didn't volunteer."

"Then how can you use him?"

"When we learned, through an intercept of mail coming

to Rafe Santana from Mexico, he was a friend of a girl who had a relatively high position with Mexx, it was decided he might be used."

"So everything was a setup? His transfer here?"

Kipling said, "Yes. Not that he isn't a capable man, but if his longtime friend, Susan Cereza, hadn't suggested she'd be able to get him an interview with the Mexx leaders if he came to Mexico . . . well, he'd still be 'Lightside' man back in Greater Los Angeles."

Less spoke more slowly. "What exactly is Rafe being used for?"

"I . . . the reason I made up my mind to talk to you . . . There's nothing I can do officially . . . but possibly you—"

"What? What the hell is it?"

"There's a thing called an implant-bomb." Kipling was looking down into the bath pit. "It can be controlled from a distance. When Rafe Santana is in the middle of that Mexx gathering, with Carregador and Gomes and the rest . . . then the bomb will be triggered."

Less sat silently, watching him. After a long while he said, "How did you ever get to the place where you could okay something like that?"

CHAPTER
EIGHTEEN

On the tiny screen Mr. Giggle was standing next to a flag-pole on which hung the blue and gold flag of the Republic of Southern California. "If I might abandon my familiar clown guise for a moment," he was saying, "and speak to you as plain ordinary Mr. Giggle. I've seen a good deal of this war and I know there's nothing cheers the men up like entertainment. That's why the Show Biz Fund is—"

Click!

Rafe, on his latest prowl around the villa's vast recroom, turned off the floating television set. They'd brought McRobb back to handle the War Desk. McRobb and Mr. Giggle in the same half hour were more than Rafe was in the mood for tonight.

"Should have heard from her by now," he said aloud. "She's been gone the whole day."

He wasn't certain he'd hear from Susan again. Someone else would probably come for him here. Rafe knew she'd be at the upcoming Mexx gathering, though. He'd see her then.

"And after that?"

Seven years go by and you realize you still love the girl.

"You ought to have figured that out back then and saved everybody a lot of trouble."

No, it had to go this way. She had to come back to Mexico, he had to rise in the employ of the Republic of Southern California News Network.

"Seven years, though. Why'd you wait—"

Rattle! Clatter! Rattle!

A big noise from the upper living room.

Rafe went running up the ramp.

"Dimwit, you nearly tossed me," someone was complaining in a fluting voice. "Wait until I get a chance to make some adjustments on you."

"A million expressions of grief and chagrin, sahib."

"What a lousy situation, having to depend on an NRA wheelchair."

"Who might you be?" Rafe asked of the plump, crippled young man he found in the center of the one-way neoglass room.

Crackpot gave his new, and inferior, wheelchair a smack with his functional hand. "I'm Lewis Arundel."

Frowning, Rafe moved nearer. "Did Susan send you?"

"I know all about her. I'm not, however, from Mexx."

Realizing the ramp he'd just jogged up was the only entrance to the room, Rafe inquired, "How exactly did you get in here?"

"Same way I got out of the ambush the NRA set for me," said Crackpot. "I teleported."

Rafe sat down in a floating lucite wing chair. "Nobody can teleport. Even NRA hasn't worked out—"

"Snuff NRA. I could build a functioning teleporter tomorrow, but why have all the dimwits of the world popping around even faster than they do now?" He wiped perspiration from his plump cheeks. "I didn't do it with mechanism. I have the ability to move myself through space. That's not what I came to talk about, Santana."

"No?"

"Maybe you're familiar with my nickname. I'm Crackpot."

"Crackpot? Yeah, I've heard of you, but why—"

"I identify myself to establish I'm not on the other side."

"The other side of what?"

Crackpot shifted, with some effort, to a slightly more comfortable position in his newly acquired wheelchair. "Had to abandon my own chair when those NRA goons descended on me," he said. "Too much trouble trying to teleport it out from a distance. Besides, my first concern was . . . let's get to your problem."

"I thought you concentrated on harassing National Robot & Android. How do I figure into that?"

"Try to curb your newshawk habit of interrupting with questions," Crackpot told him. "There'll be plenty of time in the hours ahead for me to give you my philosophy. Right now—"

"I'm waiting to start an assignment, Lewis."

"You're waiting to get your keaster blown off."

"What do you mean?"

"I mean, Santana, you're a walking boobytrap, a living ambush, a human bomb," piped Crackpot. "I mean, you poor dimwit, they've rigged you to explode once you get close enough to Carregador."

Rafe started to reply, then stopped. He stood up, rubbed at his back. "Yeah, that's what they did at the Med Wing," he said, almost remembering. "Some kind of implanted bomb? I've never heard of anything like that."

"Of course you haven't, simp. The Republic doesn't hand out press releases on its trickier stuff."

Rafe paced, noticing he was stepping a little gingerly. "Is it timed, or can they set it off?"

"They set it off. They also know where you are now, thanks to a simple monitoring device built into the thing," explained Crackpot. "Gives them chiefly locations. They're not getting our conversation or even the fact I'm here talking with you."

"This whole business then, my promotion, the chance to work in Mexico," said Rafe. "None of it had anything to do with me."

"Only in as much as you happened to be a friend of Susan's and she happened to be tied up with Mexx."

"So they did divert her letters." Rafe carefully sat again. "Damn, they're trickier than I thought, and I've been on the inside of things."

Crackpot laughed a snickering laugh. "You've only just reached a conclusion I came to when I was eleven," he said. "It's an even lousier world than you've been led to believe. Okay, now we'll rent a skycar and go see a friend of mine in Durango."

"What for?"

"To get that bomb out of your hide, dimwit," said Crackpot. "Or were you planning to go ahead and blow up?"

"What about Susan? She's sending someone to—"

"Forget about romance until the bomb's removed, Santana. The safest procedure is to have my friend take it out surgically."

"But I ought—"

"You ought to get your head out of your butt and do what I tell you," said Crackpot.

CHAPTER
NINETEEN

Strange and unfamiliar odors drifted across the night to Perdido. He wiped at his nose with his metal hand as he hurried up the ramp to the cluster of buildings he sought.

Just-Like-Home Lodge!

Vacationing Service Men Welcome!

Complete American Atmosphere & Menu!

Most Americanized Lodgings in Annexed Mexico!

Last Chance for American Style Life Before War Zone!

The neoglass and synwood front of the main lodge was rich with lightstrip signs. Sitting on a floating porch in an antique tube-rocker was a motherly looking person in shawl and flowered shift.

"Well sir, sonny, welcome to Just-Like-Home," greeted the gray-haired motherly person. "Sit yourself down a spell, take a load off your dogs. We'll have us a little gabfest before we get you all registered and tucked in for the night."

Perdido came hurrying up the ramp. The smells pouring out of the scent-nozzles over the arched entrance made his nose wrinkle. "Listen, *mamacita*, I'm no gringo soldier. I came to see—"

"Ah, our down-home food smells are getting to you, laddy, bringing a tear to your eye. Yessir, we got frozen waffles a-thawing, we got poptarts in the toaster, we got frozen pizza wedges in the radar range, we got—"

"Stuff all that." Perdido pointed his metal forefinger at the motherly person. "I got to see Mr. Fourteen. It's urgent, crone."

"Ain't that an odd name, sonny? Hardly friendly sounding." After a bit more rocking, the motherly person said, "We also got instant carobcocoa steaming in big hefty pseudopewter mugs. Sure you wouldn't—"

"I have to see this Fourteen *cabron!* Get him or I'll toast your—"

"Easy, jerko, or you'll unseat my wig."

Perdido let go. "You're not no old lady."

"Right, and unless you give me the correct password, Perdido, you'll be the one with toasted—"

"Wait a minute, *momentito*." He rubbed his metal fingers along his side. "Oh, yeah, I remember it. 'I never met a man I didn't like.'"

"That's her for sure, sonny. Why you in such an all-fired hurry to see Fourteen anyway?"

"Listen, I shouldn't even be here in Laverga. But I thought I better let them know things are going wrong." He leaned closer to the rocker. "Fourteen has got to put me through to Edgar Allan Boskow and those guys back in Guaymas. Are you Fourteen?"

"Would I be sitting out here dressed up like an old bimbo if I were? Nope, I'm Seventy-Six."

"Is that how it works? The larger the number the lower your rank? Seems to me—"

"What do you have for Boskow?"

"I'm not going to spill it to a Seventy-Six."

"See? See how your attitude changed once you became aware—"

"Get me to Fourteen quick."

Seventy-Six patted his gray wig. "Go on in the main entrance there, turn left just beyond the bowling alley, go along the ramp until you pass the fried chicken shack and then knock on the door marked 14."

"He's got his number on the door? That's not my idea of secr—"

"No, no, that really is room 14. Fourteen is in there entirely by coincidence."

"Okay, I'll go see him."

"Can't you even give me a hint as to what's gone blooey now?"

Perdido flashed him the metal finger and rushed inside.

". . . bodies dot the dry fields, the bodies of young men who until this pitched battle for Position 31 were alive and now are dead as—"

Buzz! Butz! Buzz!

Edgar Allan Boskow dropped his dicmike to the thermal rug. "Always I get interrupted in the middle of a damn simile," he said to himself. "What kind of horsepuckey do they want to drop on me now?"

Buzz! Buzz!

The burly war correspondent rolled aside a specially fitted section of the yellow rug, stomped on a concealed button. A secret pixphone unit rose up out of the floor of his room. "What now?" he demanded of the face looking anxiously out of the screen. "Who the puckey are you?"

The man was short, dark and in need of a shave. "I'm

Fourteen. We met at the Covert & Clandestine Ball last winter in—"

"You were Seventeen then."

"I've been promoted. I'm heading up things here in Laverga, and apparently mine was one of the emergency names you gave an informant of yours, not my name but my number rather. At any rate, to make a long story short and not take up any more of your time than necessary, since I'm certain you're as busy as—"

"You got Perdido there?"

"Yes, that's the name the young man is using."

"Put him on."

"Then it's all right with you if we allow him to use our communications sys—"

"Put him on."

"Hi, Boskow," said Perdido when he'd replaced the image of Fourteen. "Here's something you better know. Rafe Santana's missing."

"Huh?" Boskow gave his beard a few tugs. "He's not missing. He is, according to our tracking monitor, on his way to Durango or thereabouts."

"Well, that could be," said Perdido. "The meeting, though, is going to take place about fifty miles from here at 5 A.M."

"Not in Durango or thereabouts?"

"No, *jefe.*"

"Then why the frap is Rafe going in the other direction?"

"*Quien sabe?*" Perdido gave a shrug. "Susan sent a man to gather him up a couple hours ago. When the guy got to where Rafe was supposed to be, he wasn't."

"You're absolutely certain they're going to meet near where you are now?"

"Yes. Gomes is already there and Carregador is due at about 3 A.M. They're going to have that meeting come 5 A.M., with or without Rafael Santana."

Boskow twisted new curls into the end of his beard. "You're going to be at the meet?"

"Sure, I'm an important man in Mexx, like I told you when we made our deal," grinned Perdido. "As important as Susan."

"Okay, then you wait there in Laverga. I'll have one of our field men contact you to work out the alternative steps we're going to have to take."

"I can't hang around too long, *jefe*. They're going to wonder what I'm doing away so long as it is."

"Only a bit longer, Perdido," Boskow assured him. "Put Fourteen back on."

"All right, I'll stay a little while. *Adios*."

"Can I be of some further use?" asked Fourteen.

"I'm sending a field man to you, Fourteen. Meanwhile will you initiate Procedure 72-S."

Fourteen blinked. "72-S?"

"That's correct, yes. Bye." As soon as the screen went blank Boskow made a call. "Get me Surgical Emergency," he told the ball-headed robot who answered.

CHAPTER TWENTY

"But this is obviously of no interest to you."

"Sure, it is," said Rafe, eyes on the dark road he was guiding their rented landcar along.

"The newshound's curiosity." Crackpot was in the back seat, sitting somewhat awkwardly. His wheelchair was traveling in the luggage bin. "I forgot, Santana, you've learned to feign interest in anything."

Rafe said, "Tell me or don't tell me. Your choice."

"We've a few more miles to go. I'd rather talk about myself than listen to you moon about that Cereza girl," said Crackpot. "That's one thing I've never had to worry about . . . I've never been in love."

"I know. Is this the turnoff?"

"That should be obvious."

After executing the turn Rafe said, "You were telling me about the accident, Lewis."

"I don't really remember much about it. I was too young." He was having some difficulty breathing. Shifting and grunting, he got himself into a new position. "What I do know is we used all National Robot & Android robots in that particular wing of the plant, including their much-touted safety guard 'bots. I never would have had my fall, none of the rest of it would have happened if it hadn't been for NRA."

A silence filled the swift-moving car.

"Well?" asked Crackpot after a moment. "Aren't you going to make the obvious remark. That's why I'm doing what I'm doing. Revenge against NRA for the childhood accident."

"Nothing is that obvious."

"Maybe not to a dimwit like you, Santana," said Crackpot. "At any rate, I made up my mind then to improve all the equipment we were using. That accident gave me my vocation. When I developed the Gadget, I decided to let it loose in the world. I created a sort of underground of selected misfits and underside people all over the world. I passed out Gadgets and plans, told them how to use the thing against National Robot & Android. I called myself Crackpot. The nickname is my own, did you know that?"

"I figured."

"Oh, really? How'd you make such a bright deduction?"

"You probably never let anyone get close enough to you to give you a nickname."

Crackpot laughed his snickering laugh. "I guess my Cousin Roger was about as close as anyone," he said. "He sold me out. So you can see what closeness does for you."

"You've got to get close to more people than one, that's not a wide enough sampling."

"How about you, Santana? You have a wide circle of

close buddies, friends all over the place. Yet you got sold out same as me."

"I don't know," said Rafe, watching the night unfold, "I'm any closer to anyone than you are, Lewis."

"Not even Susan?"

"Susan may be an exception," Rafe answered. "What about this other stuff, your ability to teleport, to get glimpses of the future?"

Crackpot took a deep wheezing breath. "I kept quiet about that for years," he said. "In fact, you're about the only person who knows for sure. It wasn't too long after my accident that I started getting these little flashes of the future, pictures of things that were going to happen. Some kind of compensation maybe. When I was in my early teens I discovered I could move objects simply by willing it. Nobody to talk about that talent with either. I kept working on my machines and mechanisms, but I also practiced. Had a lot of time alone, and I never sleep much. About two years ago I learned, if that's the apt word, how to move myself from place to place. Funny, isn't it? While I can't move like most people, I can move in ways no one else can."

"Should be the ranch house up ahead," Rafe said.

"Right, that's where I told Dr. Trego to meet us," said Crackpot. "One of several places I own which no one knows about. Complete mechanical staff. We should have enough time for Trego to work on you before the assorted Republic goons start closing in."

"This isn't part of your anger at NRA." Rafe swung the landcar off the road onto a narrower drive. The lights of a large adobe house showed a quarter mile straight ahead. "Why are you mixing in Republic affairs?"

"Isn't saving your life motive enough, Santana?"

"Is it?"

"I tell you," said Crackpot, "I've been getting more and more of these damn flashes about events having nothing to do with me or National Robot & Android. Visions of lousy things the Republic is doing to people like you. At first I let them pass, ignored them. Now, though, I feel I ought to do something . . . ought to use my talents for something better than clowning."

A night-colored robot stepped up to their car as Rafe parked it near the big ranch house. "Nature of visit," said the robot in a voice very like Crackpot's.

"It's me," announced Crackpot from the back seat.

"Ah, so it is." The robot thrust a metal hand in through the open window. The hand began making sniffing sounds, a thin beam of light shot out to probe at Crackpot's puffy eyes. "Yes, sir, you check out."

"There's only one Crackpot in this world."

The robot opened the rear door.

"Is Dr. Trego here?"

"Yes, sir. Arrived minutes ago, passed all identification rituals. Some of the boys are helping him ready the medical room."

"You've got an operating room here?" Rafe stepped out into the night.

"One of a dozen facilities," answered Crackpot. "Also have a complete gourmet kitchen."

The robot reached in, slid arms under Crackpot's plump body. "Have you inside in a jiffy, sir."

"Very good. While Trego's working on you, Santana, I think I'll . . . Oh, Hell!"

The black robot had him out of the car. "Have I hurt you?"

Crackpot was breathing in short gasps. "Oh, Hell." His eyes were shut, his head shaking. "They're all going . . . all going to blow up . . . I didn't . . ."

Rafe was beside them. "What is it?"

Slowly Crackpot opened his eyes. "I just got another look ahead . . . they're going to destroy Carregador and the rest anyway."

"How?"

"Very simple. They're sticking an implant-bomb in some-one else."

"It isn't—"

"No, it's a young guy, Mexican with a metal hand."

"Must be Perdido," said Rafe. "Susan's going to be at that meeting. We've got to—"

"Wait," said Crackpot. "Let me . . . yeah, I'm getting more. The meeting is . . . in the mountains beyond a town called Laverga. Going to take place at five this morning. Unless I can stop it everybody's going to die."

"Laverga's a hundred miles south of here," said Rafe. "We'll need a skycar."

"Dr. Trego arrived in a skycar, sir," supplied the robot. "It's concealed in the barn."

"Rafe," said Crackpot, "you stay here, let Trego remove that gimmick from you. I'll fly myself to—"

"No, I'm going along."

Crackpot said, "Okay, we won't argue. I . . . maybe I can do something for you. Right now, though, let's get to that skycar."

The robot, carrying him like a child in its arms, went trotting toward the barn.

CHAPTER TWENTY-ONE

Clifford Less yawned. He yawned once more before pushing the knob of the Gadget he was carrying. The lightstrips in the underground corridor flickered, came to life. The weary-looking Regional News Chief was in the bowels of the Vista De Pajaro cantina. He'd been tipped by Oscar Kipling that he could find out exactly where Rafe Santana was from the tracking monitor down here in this hidden Republic intelligence center. Kipling wouldn't provide any passwords or entry codes, but the Gadget Less had bought last month had got him this far in.

He knew there was only a mechanical staff on duty this late at night.

He was passing among them now, large humanoid robots and worker androids. They manned the various coding, tracking, monitoring and bugging instruments in the neoglass rooms on each side of the long twisting corridor.

The ribbed noryl plastic floor slanted downward. At its end was a solid metal door marked MONITOR 6.

"This is the place." Less poked another button on the white sphere.

The door whispered open. The robots and androids in here were still, offshift. Only one mechanical man was at work, the headless tank-shape robot who was sitting at the monitoring unit which was tracking Rafe.

"Please, may this humble personage request that you shut the door, sahib," spoke the robot out of its midsection voice-hole. "The draft gives one a chill."

Less let the door close. "I want a location on Rafe Santana," he said as he weaved through the sundry machines and silent robots.

"What is your authorization, effendi?"

Less depressed a new combination of buttons.

Thung! Bong!

"Hey, don't go breaking that damn machine."

"Forgive me, bwana, I was merely bowing to your infinite worth and mastery of—"

"Where's Santana?" Less stopped at the headless robot's side.

One of its several arms swung up, pointed at the screen of its monitoring unit. A section of map glowed there, and moving very slowly across it was a minute red dot. "Subject Santana, after a pause in the vicinity of Durango, is now heading in this direction."

An abundance of new wrinkles formed on Less' forehead while he scanned the map. "Could be he's going to Laverga," he said. "The mountain country around there would make for a nice secluded meeting ground."

"A similar conclusion passed through the miserable brain of this vastly inferior person, sahib."

"So he's going to Laverga after all, huh? Well, we'll have two blowups instead of one."

Less turned. "Evening, Boskow."

Edgar Allan Boskow, beard seeming to bristle and crackle, came striding into the room. "How'd you find out about this place?"

"From a reliable source," answered the news chief. "I also know you're working for somebody besides us."

Boskow was holding a blaster pistol. "You haven't been a bad boss, Clifford," he said, moving nearer. "You never shoveled on the horsepuckey as thick as some of—"

Bong!

The gun leaped from Boskow's fist, went spinning, hit a wall, bounced off a bugging co-ordinator and landed with a whack on the smooth floor.

One of the big silent robots had come alive to bop the bearded correspondent on the skull with a large metal fist.

Boskow slapped the floor a second and a half after his weapon.

Less gave the Gadget in his hand a weary smile. "Like to meet the guy who thought this up." He made his way out of there.

"No, really, gosh, I ought to know what I ordered. Yes, and it was definitely 'Highlights of the Inquisition.' What I seem to have unfolding before me is something which might be 'The Betty Boop Festival.' Hardly, you know, the same thing." Howie Peet, bouncing discontentedly in a near-leather slingchair, was talking to the pixphone and watching the viewscreen of the giant TV set which floated in the middle of the media pit.

The desk clerk robot's head was turning deeper and deeper shades of pink. "I am most disturbed at this, sir," it said. "We pride ourselves here at the Posada Sombra in having one of the finest select-vision systems in the world.

We offer the widest vidisc selection in the Americas, indeed in—"

"Golly, I don't want to get you all frazzled down there," said the young Director of the United Federation Secret Police. "I mean, the thing is, I'm pretty darn excited about all the special interest shows you offer on your select-vision system, a catalogue for which I happened to find in the same drawer with my Gideon Bible. I've checked off quite a few I wanted to catch during my stay. This . . ." Peet, bouncing, lifted the thick open catalogue off his lap. "Yes, this 'Aspects of the Chinese Water Torture' sounds like it should be terrific, and 'The Cat-O-Nine-Tails in Lore & Legend' is—"

"Sir, we'll have our sleek and efficient repair team up to your villa in moments. Meantime, I suggest you adjourn to your balcony to enjoy a pleasant nightcap courtesy of the Posada Sombra."

"Hot carobcocoa'll be swell." Setting the catalogue aside, Peet left the pit and walked out onto the long wide balcony. Something made him glance to his right. "By golly, how are you?"

Sitting forlornly on the neighboring balcony, with a mug of nearbeer in his hand, was Arnold Bennish, the National Robot & Android troubleshooter. "Go away," he said.

"Feeling glum about something, Arnie?"

The valet 'bot rolled out onto the balcony with a mug of carobcocoa on a silver tray. "On the house, marse."

"Don't call me, Arnie. Don't, in fact, address me at all."

After thanking the servo, Peet bounded over to the rail which divided his balcony from the troubleshooter's. "Golly, the last time I saw you, Arnold, you were sitting on top of the world. You vowed to bring in that Crackpot fellow and—"

"I didn't. He got clean away. I didn't catch him."

"Got away? Gosh, how?"

"Magic."

Peet chuckled. "Now, Arnold, there's no such thing as magic. I think if you study your problem in a realistic—"

"I've been studying my problem in a realistic way, Howie. There's no way Crackpot could have escaped from that frapping landvan. Nevertheless, he did. His cousin couldn't tell me anything more. Crackpot was coming down here to Mexico to help some greaseball newscaster named Rafe—"

"Santana." Peet, spilling cocoa, was hopping on one foot and then the other. "Well, golly, Arnie, I know just about where Rafe Santana is. Will that help you any?"

Bennish abandoned his nearbeer and leaped over the railing onto Peet's balcony.

CHAPTER
TWENTY-TWO

"You Mexicans really know how to season food."

"We're all great guitar players, too."

Crackpot, slumped in the passenger seat of the borrowed skycar, was munching on some instant tamales he'd found in the food locker. "You're a very difficult guy to compliment, Santana," he complained in his high piping voice.

"Yeah, that's true." They were still twenty miles from Laverga. The ship didn't seem to him to be making very good time. "Do you think you can lead us right to the meeting site?"

"I'm anticipating another vision of some sort." Crackpot licked sauce off the thumb of his good hand. "That aspect of my talent I still can't completely control." He gave a harsh sigh, twisted, moved himself so he could get a better view of

Rafe in the pilot seat. "The bomb you're carrying. I can't be sure it won't go off when the other one does."

"At about five this morning?"

"In roughly three hours, right."

"We've got to warn the guerrillas before we do anything about this thing they planted in me. That's more important than—"

"Nonsense, your own life is more important than anyone else's. Don't start sounding like one of your news editorials." He took a breath, body shaking. "Listen, Santana, I think possibly I can deactivate the bomb in your back. Deactivate and remove it, using my telekinetic abilities."

"Why'd we need Dr. Trego then?"

"Doing it surgically, getting a look at it with an X ray, would be safer," replied Crackpot. "You've been around me long enough to know I'm not handicapped by false modesty. When I say I think there's a possibility, that's exactly what I mean. I'm not one hundred per cent certain." He paused to take another wheezing breath. "Want to try?"

"Right now?"

"As good a time as any."

Rafe grinned. "If you're not successful the thing'll go off."

"That could happen."

"And this bomb was designed to kill not only me but everybody in my vicinity," said Rafe. "Meaning if I go, so do you."

"I've considered that."

"So now you're the one willing to make a sacrifice."

"Look at it this way, Santana. I don't know exactly when you may go off. Should you go blam while I'm with you, that's the end of Crackpot as we know him. Using my telek powers now actually gives me better odds than waiting it out. Want to try?"

Rafe watched the dark morning down below. "If we blow up now, then no one can warn Susan."

"True, but you haven't any guarantee they won't trigger

the bomb while we're still trying to find the guerrillas," pointed out Crackpot. "My way, the odds are a little better."

Rafe said, "Okay, go ahead."

"In the event this doesn't work, Trego will be out a sky-car, too." Crackpot finished the last tamale, wiped his finger-tips across his plump stomach. "You Latins are supposed to be devout. Want to mumble any prayers before—"

"Just proceed, Lewis."

Crackpot touched the tip of his tongue to his upper lip, eyes gradually closing. "Give me a glimpse of the damn thing," he urged himself. "A good look, not so fuzzy. Yeah . . . good . . . that's what it looks like, huh?"

Listening to Crackpot's wheezing, Rafe became more aware of his own breathing. It ceased being automatic, he had to concentrate on drawing in air and expelling it.

Crackpot had slumped farther down into the chair. "Ah . . . the little dornik on the side will trigger it if anyone tries to remove it prematurely . . . nasty touch . . . they really don't care about your well-being, Santana . . . have to . . ." His fist whitened, his eyelids pressed tighter shut. ". . . first thing to do then is . . . incapacitate that thing . . . Come on, come on . . . less stalling around . . . Do I have powers or don't I? . . . That's it . . . easy now . . . easy . . . hell!"

Rafe stiffened, expecting an imminent explosion. Nothing occurred.

"It's okay . . . I got it . . . got it." Crackpot opened his hand, held it palm upward. "Now let's have it . . . right now."

A grinding pain started in Rafe's back. "Did you get the damn thing?"

"No tougher than pulling teeth." A silver capsule less than an inch long rested in Crackpot's pale perspiring hand. "Reminds me of a Mexican jumping bean I had in my youth."

Rafe was having difficulty seeing. "I feel somewhat odd."

"Shock, after effect." Crackpot's eyes closed again.

"There's a hole where this was, but it should heal on its own. Can you handle the skycar?"

"Yeah, the fuzziness is passing," he said. "Thanks, Lewis."

Crackpot was holding the tiny implant-bomb between thumb and forefinger. "Very crude," he remarked. "I could get the same results with half the size."

The guns didn't move.

"They're waiting for me, expecting me," Rafe said again in Spanish. It was well after 4 A.M. "Tell Susan I'm here."

There were three guerrillas, each with a blaster rifle aimed at him. They'd appeared from out of the woods very soon after Rafe had set the skycar down and climbed out. It had taken longer than he'd expected for Crackpot to get any kind of telepathic fix on where exactly the meet was being held. There wasn't, therefore, much time left.

"If you have some business with such a person," said one of the men, "you can identify yourself."

"I'm Rafe Santana."

"But you cannot identify yourself."

"What do you mean? I can show you my ID packet."

All three shook their heads. "That is not the way to identify yourself," said the spokesman. "You obviously do not know how."

"I was supposed to wait at the Posada Sombra," Rafe said. "Susan was to send somebody to get, to bring me here."

"Ah, then you should have waited."

Crackpot was still inside the skycar, with his door hanging open. "Although I'm not very good with our ancestral language, Santana," he piped, "I get the impression you're not convincing these guys."

"There must be some kind of password or identifying phrase," Rafe said over his shoulder. "Maybe the damn guy Susan sent to the *posada* was supposed to give it to me."

"We're losing time."

Rafe told the three Mexx guards, "One of you go back to the meeting, tell Susan that I'm here. That Rafe is here. You've got to tell her. There's going to be an explosion."

"What's that you say?"

"A bomb's going to go off at your meeting. It's going to kill everyone near it," said Rafe. "You've got to get hold of a guy named Perdido. He's the one with—"

"You're suggesting Perdido is a traitor? A man who lost his hand defending—"

"Perdido is not only a traitor, he's a walking bomb. Damn it, believe me. They've implanted a bomb in him. It's due to go off in minutes unless—"

The ground shook, the trees rattled. Twists of branches went climbing up into the dawn, lit by flame. Smoke spewed.

Rafe sagged. "Damn, we're too late." He turned to Crackpot.

Crackpot was no longer there in the skycar.

CHAPTER
TWENTY-THREE

The first birds of the day had been starting their singing in the woodlands which surrounded the mountain clearing. Susan, after one more look at the path which led to this gathering place, had seated herself in the first circle of guerrilla leaders. There were twenty-five people here, mostly men.

Across from the dark-haired girl, legs tucked under him on the ground, Perdido had been sitting. He smiled, rubbing at the side of his nose with his metal forefinger. "What can have become of your gringo? He seemed so eager to be with you, so anxious to bring the truth to the gringo public. Can it be—"

"Enough," Gomes told him. A large fat man with, as always, a three-day growth of beard, was next to Susan. To the girl he said, "You have no idea what's happened to Santana?"

"No, none," she answered. "When Janeiro went to the Posada Sombra to fetch him, Rafe was gone. His robot-camera was still in his villa, but there was no sign of him, no message."

"It's possible," suggested Gomes, "the Republic was trailing him."

"I don't think so. If that were the case, they would have let him come to us and followed him all the way here."

Gomes nodded. "There is also the chance he's on their side."

"Not Rafe."

"I know you're fond of him. Maybe because of his fondness for you he decided he could not go through with some plan they—"

"He's not on their side. And he wouldn't simply leave the Posada Sombra without some word to me."

A tall weathered man of forty had joined the circle. It was Carregador. He lit one of his long black syngars, glancing around him. "Apparently, we're going to do our talking without benefit of cameras."

"I'm sorry," Susan said to him. "I had—"

All at once Perdido jerked to his feet, scattering gritty dust. Walking in uneven steps, running, stumbling, he deserted the group. He trotted, as though he were being pulled, across the clearing and into the woods.

Carregador rose, slowly. "What's he up to?"

They could hear the dry leaves crackling, the fallen branches snapping as Perdido went hurrying farther from them.

Then the explosion came roaring out of the woods.

"I'm too late." Clifford Less saw the flames and smoke come burning up through the morning.

With a weary sigh he punched out a landing pattern on

the control board of his skycar. He'd been circling this area around Laverga for nearly an hour, while the night thinned away and the daylight took over.

Until the explosion he'd spotted nothing. No sign of any kind of gathering, no lights, no fires.

"Poor Rafe," said Less. "I should have known more about what's been going on. I should have been on top of things."

The ship sat down in a rocky field a quarter mile from the burning section of woodland.

Less remained in his seat. "You better go out and take a look," he told himself.

"In awhile, in awhile," he answered.

The Mexx guards forgot about him. They went running for the site of the explosion.

Rafe followed.

There seemed to be trees tight in all around the spot where the fire was burning.

"Why would they be meeting in among the trees like that?" Rafe said aloud while he ran.

"They weren't, dimwit."

There was Crackpot, sprawled on his side, one shoulder against a tree. "Then Susan's okay?"

"Unless she succumbed to surprise," Crackpot said, his breathing wheezy.

"What did you do?" Rafe realized it was all right to stop, there was no urgency now.

"Well, first off I teleported myself out of our besieged car. I dumped myself here. Can you prop me up against this tree trunk? I didn't land exactly right."

Rafe genuflected, got the fat young man into something like a sitting position.

"I concentrated on our friend Perdido," continued Crackpot. "I willed him to get up and leave the others. I knew, I had a very strong feeling, the bomb was about to be triggered. So I caused Perdido to go for a tramp in the woods."

"The bomb was still inside him when it went off?"

"Unfortunately for him it was."

Rafe said, "You could have removed it, the way you got mine."

"Possibly," admitted Crackpot. "There wasn't much time. I chose the safest way. Not safest for Perdido, but for Susan and Carregador and the rest of them. He'd tried to sell them out, remember?" Crackpot shook his head. "I played this the way I thought best, Santana, I haven't got any apologies to make."

Rafe stood back from him. "I'm going to find Susan," he said. "Want me to take you someplace?"

"You ought to know by now I can move myself if need be," Crackpot said. "I'll rest here under the greenwood tree for a spell before materializing in the guerrilla encampment. Carregador, once you've explained all I've done for him, will want to shake my hand."

"That he will." Rafe left him and continued through the morning forest.

CHAPTER
TWENTY-FOUR

"Gosh, it's only air currents."

"No, it's you. It's the continual jiggling and fidgeting you do."

Howie Peet, Director of the United Federation Secret Police, pouted. "Now you're quarrelsome again, Arnold," he said. "I mean, I'm doing you several favors. Telling you almost exactly where Santana should be, after using my influence with—"

"Yeah, I'm grateful, Howie," said the NRA troubleshooter. "Let me concentrate on flying this crate."

"Not exactly a crate, it's the latest UFSP model. Actually I should be piloting it. The regulations are fairly—"

"There! There's a skycar landed in that field."

"Gosh, you're right." Peet's hands clapped together. "The

secret place for the guerrilla meeting must be right around here." Squinting at the early morning, he made an unhappy tisking sound. "Oops, Arnold, I think we're maybe going to be too late."

"Huh?"

"Well, see over there in the woods. All that smoke billowing up. Pretty much like the aftermath of an explosion, wouldn't you say?"

Bennish jabbed out a landing pattern. "If Crackpot was with Santana, close to him, then he's so much confetti now."

"Yes, that's so."

"All I have to do is make certain that scum did go sky high." Bennish chuckled as their skycar landed near the one Rafe and Crackpot had used.

Peet said, "I'm sure glad you're pleased. I wish, though, we'd have arrived in time to see the actual blowup. This whole concept of an implant-bomb is really exciting to me, you know. Gosh, there are all sorts of ways UFSP could use—"

"Let's take a gander inside that skycar first." Bennish tugged out his blaster pistol.

"Suits me. I'm very good at searching things. At the Secret Police Academy I got all—"

"Be quiet while we approach it." Bennish dropped to the ground.

Peet got out on his side of the Secret Police ship. Before joining the troubleshooter he stretched both arms out wide and took a deep breath. "Boy, nothing like mountain air to make a guy feel tiptop."

Bennish, slightly crouched, was staring into the empty and open skycar. "No one in there."

"What's that smell? Sort of familiar."

"Mex food," Bennish said. "Crackpot's supposed to like the stuff."

"Golly, then we can feel safe in assuming this is his . . .

hey!" Peet had been reaching for his holster. "That's strange."

"What?"

"Oh, my pistol just vanished into thin air."

"Huh?" Then Bennish's weapon popped out of his hand and into nothingness.

"Pretty spooky, isn't it?"

"Good morning, gentlemen." Crackpot was back in the skycar, sitting awkwardly in the passenger seat.

"Boy, that's an impressive trick," said Peet. "How exactly did you manage—"

"Crackpot! You didn't blow to smithereens."

"Not at all. I was resting over in the woodland glade yonder when I sensed your arrival," he said. "You are the dimwits from NRA?"

"He is," corrected Peet. "I'm the Director of the United Federation Secret Police. I wouldn't advise you to try any—"

"The safest thing for you, Crackpot," Bennish told him, "is to give yourself up."

"Going to try something," said Crackpot. "Before I pop off to visit the grateful guerrillas I'm going to send you two goons off on a jaunt." He clenched a fist.

"But I'm not associated with NR—"

Peet and Bennish disappeared from the field.

From a distance of ten yards someone cleared his throat. "Hope I'm not barging in on anything."

Crackpot, with some effort, leaned out of the cabin. "You're just in time if you're with National Robot & Android. Today's special is a trip southward."

"I'm Clifford Less, with the news network. I'm trying to find out where Rafe Santana is. Though I'm afraid I'm too late." He was watching the spiraling column of smoke.

"Relax, Rafe is alive. Thanks to me. I saved him."

"Who are you?"

"They call me Crackpot."

Less held out his hand. "I've always wanted to meet you."

"Ah, sahib, would you like me to put that back in the warmer perhaps?"

"This is sherbet, you simpleton."

"A million expressions of unworthiness, effendi."

Bong! Bong!

Slush!

"There now you've upset the teapot," said old Nelson Hackensacker, Jr. "My luncheons are becoming a source of—"

Buzz! Buzz!

The attendant robot on the right side of the old man's floating lunch table said, "I believe there is an urgent pixphone call for you, bwana."

Hackensacker spooned a little more liquid sherbet into his old mouth. "I never take calls during my luncheon."

"This one is said to be of extreme urgency."

Hackensacker closed his eyes, shutting out any view of the domed green-tinted dining pavilion and the maple trees outside in the midday sun.

Buzz! Buzz!

"All right, bring me the phone, gobbox."

"To hear is to obey."

Bong!

"Stop salaaming into the table." Hackensacker flung his spoon at the robot.

Ping!

The robot lifted the phone unit off its shelf, carried it to the table and set it down in the middle of the pool of spilled tea.

There was Bennish, framed by palm trees, staring out of the pixphone screen. "Uh . . ." he said.

"Success, Bennish," the old man said. "Vast and complete success is all I wish to hear about. Success!"

"Uh . . ." said Bennish once again.

"*Estruma em tu chapeau la la! Estruma em tu chapeau la la!*"

"What's that singing?"

"Oh, only some nearby peasants, sir."

"Happy are they?"

"I suppose. I don't speak Portuguese."

"Portuguese, you say, Bennish. I find it interesting that the peasants in the wilds of Mexico have taken to speaking Portuguese."

"Well, I'm not exactly in Mexico," explained Bennish. "Actually I'm more in Recife, Brazil."

"That certainly accounts for the Portuguese," said Hackensacker. "What exactly are you up to in Brazil, you tugmutton! Did Crackpot's trail lead you there?"

"This does have something to do with Crackpot, sir," the troubleshooter admitted. "What happened, and it's been damned extraordinary, is that Crackpot . . . he teleported us here."

"Us?"

"Howie Peet and I."

"That would be young Howie Peet, the Director of the United Federation Secret Police."

"Yeah, yeah. See, somehow Crackpot also caused most of our currency and credit cards to vanish. So at the moment we're somewhat stranded here in Recife, Brazil."

"I suggest you see if young Howie Peet is hiring, Bennish. You no longer work for National Robot & Android." He broke the connection, shoved the phone away with such force it skidded all the way off the slippery table to the floor.

"Allow me, effendi, to pick up the instrument."

"Leave it," ordered Hackensacker. "Bring me a fresh dish of sherbet. Don't toast this one."

Bong!

CHAPTER TWENTY-FIVE

These things happened at approximately the same time on June 29, 2015.

In the Connecticut Colony it was a few minutes before 9 P.M. A warm rain was falling down on Westport Shanty Town, splashing gently on the neowood slat roofs of the row of tilted shacks which hung out over the Saugatuck River.

Turkey, in a new suit of shreds and tatters, was hunched in a dry corner of his shack. "No scrap," he murmured. "It's good to be a free man again, to be able to enjoy a few of life's luxuries."

The lanky young man was alone in the dripping shack, watching one of the tri-op TV sets he'd acquired since being released from National Robot & Android.

Mr. Giggle, under a polka-dot umbrella, was occupying

the tiny projection stage. Rain materialized a few inches above the set to patter down on the tiny man. ". . . a very great honor," he was saying, "to be able to come here to the capital city of the United Federation and describe the impressive doings coming up this evening. Certainly a contrast, I can assure you, to be here amidst the glitter and pomp of the Presidential Drag Ball after having entertained for many weary weeks at the front lines down in Mexico. I'm sure my prankish little partner agrees with me. Eh, Knuckles?"

Knuckles had a plyoponcho on over his silver-plated body. He was jigging around the edge of a puddle. "Quite a bash, Giggle."

At the edges of the tri-op platform portions of people showed. They were watching a red plush ramp which passed close to the position occupied by Mr. Giggle and Knuckles.

"The guests will be arriving at any moment, ladies and gentlemen," continued Mr. Giggle from under his umbrella. "This, it goes without saying, is the biggest social event of the season here in the capital city."

"I wonder where the frapping capital is," said Turkey. "Looks like a lot of rich clucks there, plenty to moog. I've got to learn more about this United Federation setup."

"You can guess from the pleased ohs and ahs of this eager, yet respectful, crowd," said Mr. Giggle, "that the skycars of the invited guests are now starting to land on the pad immediately above us. Any second now the finely clad celebrities and political dignitaries will come parading down this ramp. Pretty exciting, isn't it, Knuck?"

"What's in this diddling puddle? I got me frigging foot stuck in something."

Mr. Giggle ignored the little andy. "Ah, yes, ladies and gentlemen, here comes the Secretary of Agriculture dressed as Mary Queen of Scots. Very charming, very charming. Right, Knuckles?"

"It's dog plop or something," Knuckles said. "You wouldn't expect dog plop to turn up on one of the poshest streets in—"

"The crowd, as you've noticed, ladies and gentlemen, is applauding at the next guest to come parading down the ramp. It's none other than Cardinal Newfound of the Gay Pentecostal Church, very cleverly got up as Joan of Arc."

"Give me a helpful tug, Giggle. I'm stuck fast in this muck."

"Wait a moment, ladies and gentlemen, I believe the presidential skycar is landing. Very shortly we—"

Pop!

Mr. Giggle, Knuckles, the red ramp, Cardinal Newfound and the capital city of the United Federation all disappeared. A dark, wide-shouldered young man seated behind a floating aluminum desk took their place.

"Good evening. My name is Rafe Santana and until recently I was employed by the Republic of Southern California News Network to report on the war in Mexico," said Rafe. "Tonight, thanks to my friend Crackpot, I'm going to tell you something about what's really going on down here south of the border. I'll start with the recent attempt to assassinate the Mexx guerrilla leader, Carregador . . ."

"This is a far cry from a rainy night's entertainment," protested Turkey. He stumbled to his feet. Slipping his new Gadget out of a ragged pocket, he poked a knob. "Let's have a new show."

Rafe stayed on the platform.

Turkey poked again.

Still Rafe.

"What is this supposed to mean? This clunk is on all the frapping stations. What's so important about the war in Mexico? Where is Mexico, for that matter?"

Turkey lunged against the shack door, pushed out into the rainy dark.

"Elsewhere," he said, "is where I'll seek a little diversion."

It was 6:12 P.M. Conservative Pacific Time when Edgar Allan Boskow fell out of his bed in the Walt Disney Memorial Hospital in the Glendale Sector of Greater Los Angeles.

A pretty Scandinavian-model android nurse had brought him his dinner a few moments before. "Yumpin yimminy, Eddie, you bane lookin' goot tonight."

Boskow's head was capped with white bandages and the beard had been shaved from the right side of his face. "How can I look good with the better part of my damn beard gone, Sonja. Stop trying to give me a line of horsepuckey," the war correspondent growled. "What about my request to be moved to a ward with live nurses and a human staff?"

"Dey bane done tol' me it's bein' considered, you bet."

"I loathe all androids and robots. A robot is what that bastard Less used to conk my skonce. An android doctor down in greaserland is the one who shaved the wrong end of my damn head in order to treat my skull fracture. And you, Sonja, are a blight on my recooperation."

"Here's your dinner, Eddie. It's real goot."

Boskow turned his half-bearded face toward the TV set which floated beside his bed. "I can tell you what my dinner is," he said. "It's Swedish meatballs again."

"Dat's all I know how to fix, Eddie. I vish you vouldn't all der time make visecracks."

"Why do you persist in sounding like the Katzenjammer Kids? That's no Scandinavian accent."

"By jimminy, it sure bane is."

"Will you please get the hell out of here, Sonja."

"You relax mit der tellywision, Eddie." The pretty android left him.

Boskow reached out to flick on the set.

There was Rafe Santana. ". . . Crackpot's invention we've been able to take over, utilizing several of the major communication satellites, most of the television sets in the Western Hemisphere. So it's no use trying to switch to another channel. We're going to continue to bring you the truth about the Mexican war. Right now we'll take up the part played by Edgar Allan Boskow, the much-respected war correspondent. I hate to admit that Boskow was a friend of mine and that I never suspected he was an agent for the Republic of Southern California's Intelligence Service. Boskow was important to the plot to assassinate the Mexx leaders since he—"

"Get off of there," shouted Boskow. "Nobody's going to expose Boskow unless it's Boskow." He made a swipe at the off switch.

He missed and went sliding out of his hospital bed.

Bonk!

Sonja found him spreadeagle on the floor when she checked on him at 8 P.M.

"How'd it come in over there, Nita?"

"Kind of blurry."

"That's your set, you dimwit quiff."

It was 6:40 Mexican Free Time and Crackpot, seated in his new wheelchair, was collecting reactions to his bootleg telecast.

"I ought to know how to keep my set shipshape," said Onita from Barsetshire, England.

"What sort of official response are we getting?"

"The Prime Minister was just on the telly, Crackpot. She says if any of these allegations are true it will bear the closest scrutiny by the surviving nations of the world. Because 'there is a way to conduct a war and a way not to conduct a war.'"

"Not a rave, but not bad."

"She also remarked that while you guys' intentions were obviously honorable, you shouldn't have resorted to taking over all the television sets to put forth your case. She sincerely hopes that won't happen again."

Crackpot's snickering laugh burst forth. "Not until we have more news to get out."

H 05

"You thriving down there, Crackpot? I mean now you're a renegade—"

"Nita, I still control the Arundel fortune. You don't really think Uncle Frank and the others can run things without my advice," he said. "The split with our soy business is only for the public, the segment of it which is intent on doing me harm."

The black girl bent, staring out of the pixphone screen. "Seems like you got a comfortable place there."

"I'm already in the process of building new underground headquarters here. Wait till you see some of the improvements . . . but I've got to make a lot more calls tonight. So get off."

"I'm interested in how you feel—"

"Snuff yourself." With his good hand he clicked her off and then punched out a call to Cleveland in the Heartland Empire.

The night sea was a deep slick black topped with white foam. Rafe came walking down the rocky path to the small beach house at a few minutes after 7 P.M.

Susan opened the door for him while he was still some yards away. "This isn't the Posada Sombra," she said, "so we're going to have to open our own doors."

"A very primitive country, Mexico," he said. Rafe took one step across the threshold and kissed her.